D0664046

# OLD BONES

# OLD BONES

## A CASEY TEMPLETON MYSTERY

RICHMOND HILL
PUBLIC LIBRARY

NOV 2 1 2014

RICHMOND GREEN
905-780-0711

TRANSFERRED
TO YRDSB

Gwen Molnar

**DUNDURN**

TORONTO

Copyright © Gwen Molnar, 2014

All rights reserved. No part of this publication may be reproduced, stored in a retrieval system, or transmitted in any form or by any means, electronic, mechanical, photocopying, recording, or otherwise (except for brief passages for purposes of review) without the prior permission of Dundurn Press. Permission to photocopy should be requested from Access Copyright.

All characters in this work are fictitious. Any resemblance to real persons, living or dead, is purely coincidental.

Editor: Dominic Farrell
Design: Courtney Horner
Printer: Webcom

**Library and Archives Canada Cataloguing in Publication**

Molnar, Gwen, author
        Old bones / Gwen Molnar.

(A Casey Templeton mystery)
Issued in print and electronic formats.
ISBN 978-1-4597-1404-5

        I. Title.  II. Series: Molnar, Gwen.  Casey Templeton
mystery.

PS8576.O4515O43 2014          jC813'.54          C2013-908368-5
                                                 C2013-908369-3

1   2   3   4   5       18   17   16   15   14

  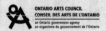

We acknowledge the support of the **Canada Council for the Arts** and the **Ontario Arts Council** for our publishing program. We also acknowledge the financial support of the **Government of Canada** through the **Canada Book Fund** and **Livres Canada Books**, and the **Government of Ontario** through the **Ontario Book Publishing Tax Credit** and the **Ontario Media Development Corporation**.

Care has been taken to trace the ownership of copyright material used in this book. The author and the publisher welcome any information enabling them to rectify any references or credits in subsequent editions.

*J. Kirk Howard, President*

Printed and bound in Canada.

The publisher is not responsible for websites or their content unless they are owned by the publisher.

Visit us at
Dundurn.com
@dundurnpress
Facebook.com/dundurnpress
Pinterest.com/dundurnpress

Dundurn
3 Church Street, Suite 500
Toronto, Ontario, Canada
M5E 1M2

*In fond memory of my siblings,*
*Helen Rodney, Barbara Ann Cram and John Ross McGregor*

*With special thanks to Robert Wuetherick for all his invaluable help.*
*And to Wendy Taylor, my gratitude for your interest and expertise.*

# CHAPTER ONE

Casey had to have it. He'd never wanted anything so much in his life. He wanted it so badly his heart was pounding and his palms were sweating.

"I'll give you thirty bucks for it." He was rubbing the curved, two-inch-long end piece of a dinosaur tooth with his thumb. Its ridged surface was cool to the touch and it fitted exactly one end of the jagged inch-long piece of tooth he'd picked up a few minutes earlier. He just had to have it.

"Fifty." Mike sounded like he meant it.

From the day Mike O'Malley had moved with his family to Richford, just two months before, he and Casey had connected as if they'd known each other all their lives. They couldn't have looked less alike: Casey, with his tumble of white-blond hair, his blue eyes, his skinny frame; and Mike, with his dark hair, freckles, deep brown eyes, and sturdy build.

"I come from Black Irish stock," he'd told Casey when they'd first met.

"What does that mean, Black Irish?" Casey had asked.

"Well, my dad says we're descended from a bunch of sailors from the Spanish Armada who got shipwrecked on Irish shores way back when. They had dark eyes and dark complexions, and black hair like me. There are a lot of other explanations as to why we're called that — I checked the web — but I'll stick with Dad's version."

"Forty," Casey offered. "It'll be all I'll have left when I've bought the stuff I want."

His parents had given him a hundred dollars spending money for this two-day field trip of Mr. Deverell's grade ten science class to the Royal Tyrrell Museum in Drumheller. Casey planned to use the rest of his money for a book on fossils, and models of two of the museum's most famous exhibits, a huge *Tyrannosaurus rex* and a not-quite-so-huge *Albertosaurus*.

The class had left Richford at 7:00 that morning for the sixty-some kilometre bus ride south. Half the class were going to be spending the field trip in and around the museum, with just an hour's "dig" each day, but the first day, Mr. Deverell had reserved ten places for his most interested students at what was called a "Day Dig" — part of the Royal Tyrrell Museum's Explorers' Program — and Casey and Mike were two of the ten.

They'd stowed their gear in the Hoodoo Hotel's locked storage room early in the morning and would be returning there at the end of the day to eat and sleep. Sometimes whole classes of students slept right in the museum, in the shadow of the gigantic dinosaurs, but other schools had booked to stay there long ago, so Mr. Deverell had reserved space for his class at the Hoodoo.

At 8:30, Casey and Mike and the other eight Richford kids met up with the Day Dig staff at the main entrance to the museum. The staff gave them a behind-the-scenes tour of the museum's fossil collection, and instructions on how they were to go about "exploring" the dig.

"Every fossil you see here," Dr. Spain, the dig's leader, told them, "was mapped and collected just the way you'll be doing it on our dig today."

A short bus ride to the quarry's parking lot, followed by a ten-minute hike up a short incline and they were at the dig site in the Red Deer River Valley.

"Can you believe," Mike asked, "this is a seventy-million-year-old rock formation and dinosaurs used to roam around here then?"

"Oh give me a home, where the dinosaurs roam," Casey whispered under his breath.

"Shush and listen," said Mike.

"The Red Deer Valley has several bonebeds preserved over an extensive area," Dr. Spain was saying. "Often the majority of the bones come from a single type of dinosaur, like the *Centrosaurus* of Dinosaur Provincial Park."

"What's in 'our' bonebed?" Casey wanted to know.

"An assemblage of 'teenage' duckbilled dinosaurs," Dr. Spain said. "And along with the juvenile dinosaurs, we've also uncovered numerous teeth from carnivorous dinosaurs such as the *Albertosaurus*."

"You must have a huge staff to cover such a big area," Mike said.

"The problem is, we don't," Dr. Spain replied, shaking his head. "And that's where teams like yours come in. By bringing in ten or twelve people each day to help, many times more work gets done. You'll be conducting real research with palaeontologists — remember what we told you this morning about how you handle what you find. As you uncover fossils at this site, you help us gain a better understanding of the dinosaurs and the other animals that lived in this area. The more we scientists know about the past, the better we're able to understand the present. End of lecture. Let's go to work."

Casey and Mike had headed away from the rest and both had got lucky.

"Give me the forty," Mike said, "and ten more when we get home, and it's yours." Mike liked science but he liked music even more — and the CDs he wanted cost fifty dollars.

"All right." Casey nodded. "My wallet's in my pack at the hotel; I'll give you the money later."

"You know you can't keep what you find anyway," Mike reminded Casey.

"I know," said Casey, "but I want to hold all the pieces of a real dinosaur tooth in my hand; and the museum will put my name as the finder on a card in that fossil room."

They worked on as the sun rose higher and higher.

After a while, Mike called to Casey. "They're going to be serving us lunch in the Museum Cafeteria at twelve." Mike was always hungry. "Let's get back to the bus and get in the shade for a while."

"Okay." Casey put his water bottle down to mark his spot.

Lunch was a better one than Casey was expecting, and being in the air-conditioned museum was a real treat. He was kind of wishing he'd opted for only the short dig, but the feel of the tooth pieces in his pocket made him decide he was glad he was going back to hunt for the rest of the tooth.

Back at the dig, Dr. Spain reminded them of the afternoon's schedule. "The bus leaves for the museum at 2:50, but you're welcome to spend the rest of the day at the museum."

Mike wanted to talk to one of the staff, so Casey went back to "his" spot alone. Before restarting his search, he took a drink of his now lukewarm water and looked around.

*This is one strange place*, he thought, *no wonder it's called the badlands*. He'd read that early French trappers and traders had called the Whiter River area of South Dakota *les mauvaises terres* — the badlands — and before them, the Sioux Indians called them *Mako Sica*, meaning "land bad." The name had stuck for all such landscapes in the western United States and in this part of Alberta.

Casey pulled his broad-brimmed hat further down on his forehead (Mr. Deverell said they couldn't go on the dig without one). Gazing over the landscape, he took another swallow of water. He remembered the moment on the ride into Drumheller when, at a turn in the road, the landscape changed from open, sweeping prairie to this enchanted, mysterious valley, with its hoodoos and mounds and hollows and hills and arroyos all carved by wind and weather. *An alien world*, Casey thought.

He got down on his knees right where he'd found his piece of tooth. *Should have worn long pants like they suggested we do*, he thought. He brushed away the dust and small stones that covered the ground; everything was dry, parched, and barren. His knees began to hurt so he took off his T-shirt and made a roll of it for a kneeler. Now his knees didn't hurt, but his back was getting the full brunt of the rays of the semi-desert sun. He knew he'd get a sunburn. With his fair skin, he always did, so he'd put lots of sunscreen on his face and neck.

*It's probably worn off by now*, he thought.

Was a sunburned back worth the chance of finding all the pieces of a real dinosaur tooth?

"Yes," he said right out loud, "it is."

Casey drank a gulp of water, now almost hot. It was very quiet as he worked alone in his area of the quarry and he jumped when a deep voice shouted across the rocks, "Casey, put your shirt back on, this sun will fry you."

"Okay," he said, watching as Dr. Spain moved away to another helper. "I'll put it on in a few minutes," he added to himself. Instead, because the sweat was trickling down from beneath his hat, he took it off, putting it on the ground, top down so the inside could dry.

As he patiently searched every inch, going round and round in ever-widening circles, Casey's mind wandered back to his family's move to Richford when his father retired from the Royal Canadian Mounted Police almost a year ago.

His parents had been so happy to return to their home-town, Richford — Paradise on the Prairies. But paradise it wasn't. This they found out when Casey, out to retrieve the antique pipe of his father's, which he'd "borrowed," had come upon a wounded Mr. Deverell who'd been left to die in a snow storm at the remote Old Willson With Two L's Place on the outskirts of Richford. Casey had discovered that the attic of the Willson house had been turned into the high-tech headquarters of a Hate Cell whose members were harassing the town's minorities.

Things had quieted down once the hate gang had been apprehended.

Mr. Deverell was almost back to being his old self, except he didn't have as much energy as he used to and got tired quite quickly. Apparently, the doctors had told Mr. D. it'd take at least a year for him to feel like himself.

Casey smiled, remembering how much his actions had helped to put the "bad guys" away. He guessed he'd never again be challenged to use his so-obviously-superior skills at detection. *Not unless I join a police force like Dad did*, he thought, *and that I don't plan to do.* Casey had long ago decided he wanted to be an archaeologist.

Continuing his inch-by-inch search, Casey found wrappers from six sticks of Juicy Fruit gum, two ballpoint pens, a dime, and three cigarette butts, but not one more piece of tooth. He stopped a minute, reached up to scratch a shoulder blade, and smiled as he thought again of his winter adventure.

While he'd ended up a hero of sorts for saving Mr. Deverell's life, and helping to solve the mystery of who was running the Hate Cell, he'd done a lot of pretty dumb things as well. As punishment, after every snowfall last winter his father'd made him clear the snow off their driveway and all the neighbours' sidewalks as well — a lot of work since it was the snowiest winter in one hundred years. *It was a typical Chief Superintendent Templeton–type punishment*, Casey thought. *One that gives the punishee lots of time to think about why they are being punished and one that keeps said punishee fit and healthy at the same time.*

*I wish there was a great big pile of that snow here right now*, Casey fantasized. *Boy, would it feel good to roll around in it.* Instead, he stood up in the hot sun and stretched.

"Someone else must have found the rest of my tooth," he muttered in frustration.

The bus horn blasted. Casey looked at this watch. Was it really already 2:50? A long time since lunch. Shaking the sand from his sweaty T-shirt, Casey pulled it over his head. His back felt a little hot, but not bad. Maybe the sun hadn't been all that powerful after all. He put on his hat, checked his pocket to make sure he still had the two pieces of tooth, and walked to the museum bus. He handed his treasures to Dr. Spain.

Looking at them closely, Dr. Spain said, "Nice find, Casey. I'm putting them in a zip-lock — see — and putting your name on it."

"Wish I could have found more." Casey sat down with a thump as the museum bus lurched to a start and started back over the bumpy road.

After an hour-and-a-half looking at fossils inside the air-conditioned Tyrrell, the ten Day Dig students joined their classmates in the school bus in front of the museum.

"Our hotel rooms will be ready when we get there." Mr. Deverell was kneeling on the front seat facing the class as the bus driver started the engine. He frowned as Casey, the last to get on, slid into the only empty seat — the one beside him. "First, get your gear from the hotel's storage room. Then assemble it in the foyer. I've made a chart of who bunks with whom and I'll give you your keys. We're all on the second floor, but we do have one small problem. We've one boy too many and the hotel has one room too few, so one of you boys will be sleeping in a closet. It's a big closet, even has a window. Do I have a volunteer?"

"I'll take the closet," Casey said. He'd brought a powerful flashlight and a favourite Harry Potter he was rereading. If he was on his own, he could close the closet door, open the window, and read as late as he wanted.

"Good lad." Mr. Deverell went on to read out the list of roommates and room numbers. "Your closet is in Mike and Kevin's room, Casey. Room 327."

Instead of eating at the Hoodoo, Mr. Deverell had arranged for the school bus to take the class to the famous Smorgasbord Night at the Badlands Motel. The dining room was packed with tourists, townspeople, and lots of visiting school kids, including the twenty-one from Mr. Deverell's science class.

# CHAPTER TWO

"I've never seen so much food on one table." Mike had managed to get first place in line.

"You don't have to try to put it *all* on your plate" — Greta Maitland frowned at Mike — "leave a little for the rest of us."

Because her father was the second-richest man in Richford and owned the Milford Mall, Greta acted as if none of the other kids was her equal. Mike just stared at her, a long silent stare, and took his plate back down the line to stand behind Casey.

"Why didn't Greta Maitland stay home?" Mike asked. "Her being here's going to ruin everything."

Casey shrugged.

"She's a large pain for sure. Only time she was ever mildly decent was when she was dating Bryan Ogilvie," he said, thinking how he'd set her up with Bryan, whose dad was even richer than Greta's. "When she and Bryan were an item, she was almost likeable."

"I never met this Bryan," Mike said. "He was off to that fancy prep school down east before I got here. What's he like?"

Casey thought for a minute. "Bryan Ogilvie is one weird dude," he said. He squelched the urge to tell Mike the whole story of Bryan's part in the hate activities that had turned Richford upside-down last fall, but Casey would never forget the way Bryan had been lured into joining the cell by Internet hate predators. Bryan got out of the mess only because Casey made him tell Casey's parents. Bryan was forbidden by the police to use the Internet for two years and had to swear he'd never call up any hate sites. "He was always a loner — not by choice though; everybody just ignored him."

"That'd be tough to deal with," Mike said.

"It was. Bryan really resented always being on the outside. He spent an awful lot of time on the net; he has an awesome computer set-up and is an absolute computer wizard."

"As good as your brother Hank?" Mike wanted to know.

"Nobody's as good as Hank," Casey told him, remembering how Hank's skills had helped solve the Hate Cell mystery.

"All that stuff Bryan's got — must'a cost a bundle," Casey continued. He could see the wheels turning in Mike's brain. "A big bundle."

"Money's no problem in the Ogilvie family," said Casey. "Bryan's dad inherited pots of dough. My folks went to school with B.O. Ogilvie — that's what they called his father — in Richford. They say all that money changed him for the worse. Bryan's father is not an easy person to like."

"So Bryan goes away and Greta's back to being Greta again," said Mike.

"Just ignore her, like the rest of us do." Casey eased himself down, being careful not to let his back touch the chair. He could feel the heat radiating through the clean white T-shirt he'd changed into for supper.

"I do," Mike said, "but she makes me feel … What are you looking at, Casey?"

"See that girl standing at the end of the supper line with the tall man in the blue shirt and the lady in beige?"

"Yeah, I see her," Mike said. "She is really tall and she is really pretty. You know her?"

"We were on the same swim club for a couple of years when I lived in Edmonton — the Green Beavers. Her name is Mandy Norman. She's sixteen now and the fastest female backstroker in the province."

"So, go talk to her."

"Yeah, I will. I got to know her pretty well even though I was only on the junior boys' relay team. Everybody liked Mandy, although she's really competitive. She just does what she does better than anybody else. I'd say she's Olympic material, but being the best didn't go to her head: When she could, she'd watch the others on the team and say something encouraging to them."

"Sounds as if you liked her," Mike said.

"Yeah." Casey looked a little sad. "She was great and I missed her. The area swim team I'm on now is fine but there's nobody on it like Mandy Norman." He turned his head and looked again at the Normans. "I even liked her mother. She and my mom got to be good friends driving us all over Alberta. I'll go talk to them when we've eaten." Casey put three chicken legs on his plate and a pile of potato salad.

"I've got all I want here," Mike said. "Let's take those two places at Kevin and Terry's table in the corner." He got Kevin's attention and waved. But they were too late. Greta Maitland and Polly Beach slid into the chairs just as Mike and Casey got to the table.

"Real sorry," Greta said, settling in. "I'm sure you'll find somewhere else to sit; that plate of yours must be awfully heavy to carry, Mike."

Kevin and Terry shrugged helplessly as Casey and Mike turned around, looking for somewhere to sit.

"There's an empty table by the kitchen door," Casey said, holding his plate high as he wove among the tables.

As they neared the table he'd spotted, a girl's voice called out, "Casey? Casey Templeton?"

Casey turned toward the voice. He hadn't heard it for ages but he knew who it was.

"Hi, Mandy. Hi, Mr. Norman," he called out.

"Gimme your plate and go talk to them," Mike said. "I'll grab the table."

Casey manoeuvred among the crowded tables.

"You guys checking out the Tyrrell?" he asked as he got to the Normans' table.

"Dad's been working there three months now," said Mandy, putting the chicken wing she was holding back on her plate. "He's executive director at the Tyrrell."

"I didn't know," Casey said. "Mom doesn't know either or she'd have said." Casey saw Mrs. Norman staring at his neck. He tried to shrug down into the rim of his T-shirt.

"I've been meaning to call your mother," Mrs. Norman told Casey, "but what with finding a house and getting settled here, I've just not done it." She was looking intently at Casey. "That looks like a bad burn you've got. Did you put some after-sun lotion on it?"

"It's fine," said Casey, knowing that it wasn't but not wanting anyone to make a fuss. "Listen. It's great to see you all but I don't want to interrupt your supper. I'll come talk to you later — catch up on all your news."

"Fine." Dr. Norman nodded. "We want to hear your news too. Come have dessert with us."

"Will do, Dr. Norman." Casey gave a wave as he found his way back to Mike.

"So, Mandy did remember you?" Mike asked, tipping back the chair he'd saved for Casey.

"Yeah." Casey smiled. "Even her mom and dad remembered me. I'm going to talk to them later."

But he never got the chance. Just as Casey put the first bite of potato salad in his mouth, the area around the Norman table erupted. People scrambled out of the way. Casey climbed on his chair. He couldn't see much, but he heard Dr. Norman call out, "Is there a doctor here?"

"What's going on?" asked Mike.

They heard soon enough. Mandy Norman had got a tiny chicken bone caught in her throat and was turning blue. Luckily, there *was* a doctor in the dining room. He managed to move the bone a little so Mandy could breathe. Soon, an ambulance arrived and the ambulance attendants rushed in to treat Mandy. They were giving her oxygen as they wheeled her out for the short drive to the hospital.

"What a crazy thing to happen," Mike said. "Poor Mandy."

"Yeah." Casey looked stricken. "I sure hope she'll be okay." He was starting to feel a little out-of-it. "I'll get in touch with her parents later. Let's eat and get out of here."

# CHAPTER THREE

Casey lay on top his unrolled sleeping bag. He'd opened the window in his closet and didn't need to look down to figure out it was right over the hotel's trash bins. His book and flashlight were on the floor beside him, but he didn't feel like reading. His back felt like it was on fire. He heard the buzz of his friends' voices in the room next door. Casey propped himself up on an elbow, glad he'd been smart enough to bring in a glass of water. He put his head back and took a long swallow. Dizziness engulfed him and everything started to spin. Water sloshed over him and his sleeping bag as the glass fell out of his hand. But Casey didn't even notice as he sank back in a dead faint.

Later, much later, Casey woke. A light above the garbage cans was flickering on and off, and the smell coming in his window made him want to throw up. He felt cold. Cold on his chest and fiery hot on his back.

He sat up cautiously, his sopping-wet T-shirt clinging to him.

"What the ...?" he whispered. The last thing he remembered was taking a drink of water. But where was the glass? And why was the water all over him? He picked up his flashlight and swung its beam slowly around the room. In the corner, across the closet, the glass lay on its side.

*I'll get it in the morning,* Casey thought. *In the meantime ...* He turned his T-shirt with the wet part to the back. The coolness felt so good on his burning skin.

Casey opened his sleeping bag, slid in, and zipped it up. He hoped none of the water had got through to the inner lining. It hadn't, and he turned on his stomach and closed his eyes.

He couldn't relax, though. The smell of the garbage came wafting up. "Darn it!" he whispered, "I meant to close the window." He unzipped the sleeping bag, crawled out, rested on his knees a while, and then stood up. He felt dizzy but managed to get to the window by supporting himself with one hand against the wall.

As he reached up to close the window, Casey heard a man's deep voice say, "I'd about given up on you. Where the heck have you been?"

The voice was coming from a room whose window was at right angles to Casey's. Because the window was at the far end of the room the voice was coming from, Casey couldn't see anything but the side of a television set that someone clicked off, and the blank wall beyond it. He listened, silently.

"I'd have stayed away longer," — the second man's voice was higher pitched — "if I'd known how much this room stinks. Why don't you close the window?"

"I tried, but it's stuck," said the first voice. "Forget the smell. Where have you been?"

"Look," said the second man, "I was having a friendly drink with some of the locals, two guys that work security for the museum. And I found out exactly what we needed to know. That area we took the video in today, where the stuff we're supposed to take is — it does have its own door to the outside. And, get this, it's not on the same alarm system as the rest of the museum, though it does have a guard night and day."

"So, when we come back for the stuff, we can put the guard out of commission and disarm that one system?" the low voice asked.

"That's what I'm saying, yeah," the second man replied.

"You figure those guys' info is reliable?" the first man wanted to know.

"Can't imagine a better source," said the second man. "I got it by talking to the guards, like I said, and buying them several rounds. Told them I was going to apply for a job in museum security."

"So that's how come they were talking so free, eh?"

"You got it," the second man agreed. "And so you had to wait a while in this smelly hole; well, that's tough."

"All right. All right. You did fine," the deep voice said. "I'm almost packed. You'd better get going. We're out of here first thing in the morning."

"When do you figure the boss'll be sending us back up here?" asked the second man.

Casey could hear him clomping unevenly back and forth. One tread light, one heavy. Casey strained to see into the room. No luck.

"You know better than to ask," the first man told him. "We'll get our orders after we're back Stateside and when we've shown him our pictures of the things he's interested in for his collection. I gotta say that fall of yours that brought the guard fussing around sure gave me a great chance to make the video. And this little camera's a wonder. Nobody even knew I had it."

"That fall really hurt! I got a bruise four inches round on my hip. And I twisted my one ankle. The boss is going to get a bill for 'pain and suffering.' I tell ya that fall was above and beyond the call of duty."

"And I tell you, when he sees them pictures he's going to give us both a bonus," the man with the deep voice chuckled.

"I'm done packing now," Casey heard the lame man say. "I'll have a shower and then hit the sack. You set the alarm?"

"Yeah," said the first man.

The television clicked on and Casey quietly closed his window.

Casey crept back to his sleeping bag. His senses were reeling as his mind bounced back and forth between the conspiracy he'd just overheard and the sickness he felt coming on. He tried to find a comfortable position, but his back was hurting so much he almost cried.

"I'm so thirsty and I feel so awful," Casey muttered to himself. He knew he was going to throw up, but he didn't want to wake the boys in the next room by going through to the bathroom. He felt around on the floor for his wide-brimmed hat and threw up in it. He felt a lot better after that, but his closet now smelled worse than the garbage.

Holding the hat in both hands, he got up shakily and walked to the window. How to open it and not spill anything? He pulled the side edges of the brim together, held the hat in his left hand and opened the window with his right, then dropped the brimming hat into the dumpster under it. As he closed the window, his eye caught a movement in the room where he'd heard the voices. The shadow of a tall, slim man appeared for a second on the wall past the television set. The shadow of a tall, slim man with only one leg.

Then, as the other man stepped forward to close the drapes, Casey caught a glimpse of his face: wavy dark brown hair above bushy eyebrows that met above frowning dark eyes.

*I'll tell Mandy's dad all about this in the morning*, Casey thought as he slipped into an exhausted sleep.

# CHAPTER FOUR

The clickety-clack of a low-flying helicopter woke Casey. He found he was lying on his back in a bed. Nothing in the room looked even vaguely familiar; in fact, the room was like none he'd ever seen. Fluffy white curtains matched the frilly skirt on a dressing table across the room. A shelf held about fifty stuffed animals. The lamp on the bedside table had a pink shade. His eyes focused on a row of trophies high on a shelf above a large desk. He recognized the biggest trophy. He'd seen Mandy Norman win it two years ago at the provincial championships: first prize for back stroke. What was he doing in Mandy Norman's bedroom?

As he tried to sit up, Casey became conscious that his upper body was bandaged and that there was the smell of some medicine in the air. He tried to remember last night. He'd said hello to the Normans, had eaten supper with Mike, and then? Oh yes; there was the fuss about Mandy and the chicken bone in her throat. He sure hoped she was all right. He hadn't gone to talk to the Normans but had headed straight to the bus, and up to his closet as soon as the bus stopped at the Hoodoo. Yes, he'd gone straight to bed. No. Not exactly. He'd opened the window but he'd been too tired to take off his clothes. He'd just pulled off his pants and laid down on top his sleeping bag. He remembered taking a drink of water; then, nothing. What had happened next, and how had he got here?

Casey swung his legs over the edge of the bed and stood up. He was planning to get Mrs. Norman to explain things, but as he took a step, he felt weak, so he flopped back on the bed and closed his eyes.

He heard steps in the hall. *It'll be Mrs. Norman*, he thought, *she'll tell me what's going on*. It was not Mrs. Norman. Casey opened his eyes to see his mother looking down at him with a worried frown.

"Hi, Mom," he said. "Why are you here?"

"Casey," said his mother, smiling but shaking her head. "You got yourself in one fine fix. Your poor back has second-degree sunburn, and you've been mostly out of it for two days with sunstroke."

"Two days!" Casey exclaimed. "You mean I've missed the rest of the field trip?"

"Mr. Deverell took the class back last night," said Mrs. Templeton.

"But I'm okay now, aren't I?" Casey asked. "Maybe you and I could do the museum tour together, Mom. You haven't seen it, have you?"

"Most of it," said his mother. "The Normans have been terrific, looking after you and making me feel so at home."

"How come I'm here?" Casey asked.

"Seems when they checked at breakfast the day after your group got here, you weren't there. Mr. Deverell found you unconscious in your closet and took you right to the hospital. You were in Intensive Care in the same room as Mandy Norman. But the second night there was a bad accident just outside of town and your bed was needed. The rest of the hospital was full, and your doctors said you'd be fine to stay with the Normans because you'd been awake off and on and your recovery was simply a matter of rest. The Normans brought you here, and phoned me."

"Mandy's still in hospital?" Casey wondered.

"Yes, but not here. A small piece of chicken bone actually tore her larynx. She's been flown to Edmonton for some very delicate surgery."

"Poor Mandy," Casey said. "She won't be able to train."

"Not for a long time," said his mother. "Now, tell me how you feel."

"Well," Casey considered. "I felt a little woozy when I tried to stand a few minutes ago. But my back doesn't burn any more." He looked around. "Where's all my stuff?"

"Your things are in the closet." Mrs. Templeton pointed to a door on the other side of the room. "Except for your hat. Didn't you even wear your hat when you were out in the sun for so long?"

"Sure, I wore it," said Casey. "And it was on the closet floor when I went to sleep. No … Wait a minute. I …"

He lay back. What had he done with his hat?

"Would you like something to eat, Casey?" his mother asked. "Weak tea and toast, or …"

"Food!" said Casey. "That's it. I threw up my supper in my hat and then I …" He stopped a minute. He could see himself with his hat in both hands. What had he done with it? "And then I dropped it into the dumpster under my window."

"Good thinking," said his mom. "So, how about it? Want something?"

"Yeah, Mom, that'd be great. Should I just stay here or come with you?"

"Stay put," she said. "I'll be back in a few minutes."

Something was nagging at Casey's mind. He remembered opening the window, remembered dropping his hat. But there was something else. He tried concentrating very hard. But instead of remembering, he fell fast asleep.

"Sit up, Casey."

As used as he was to obeying his mother's voice, Casey was finding it hard to wake up. It was the smell of warm, buttered toast that finally roused him and he did as she said.

"Now, lean forward and I'll put another pillow behind you."

"This looks good." Casey nibbled a piece of toast and then took a sip of tea. "Reminds me of when I got hit by that car when I was five and everyone was so nice to me."

"Your brothers were really worried about you," his mother said. "Hank slept on the floor of your room for three nights and Jake and Billy took turns with me sitting by your bed. Your dad was home for a time then; he didn't sleep at all."

"I didn't know that," said Casey, pausing before he bit into a third half slice of toast. "He stayed up three nights?" he asked.

That wasn't how Casey remembered his father. Actually, he hardly remembered his father at all from when he was a little kid. It was only after the family had moved to Richford that Casey and his dad began to "connect." Now, they got along well, and were slowly getting to really know each other.

"Three days and three nights; sitting outside your hospital room door. Wouldn't leave until you'd started talking. First thing you said was, 'I'm hungry.'"

"And they brought me weak tea and buttered toast."

"Right. And they brought you buttered toast at the Richford Hospital last year when you almost froze to death trying to get help for Mr. Deverell," said his mother.

"Yeah." Casey ate the last bite of toast. "I remember."

"I'll take these things away now and you can go back to sleep. The Normans say, 'Hi.' One good thing about your, ah, your condition, is that we're in contact again, and when your father gets home from the Ottawa Conference on a National Anti-Hate Strategy …"

"You haven't told him about me, have you, Mom?" Casey interrupted.

"I told him you'd got too much sun on the class field trip, and were staying at the Normans' for a while."

"And he asked, 'How much is too much?' and you told him," Casey sighed; he could just hear the lecture he was going to get.

"Well, yes," his mother admitted. "But I also told him there was no need for him to come back, that the doctors at the hospital said you'd be fine in a day or two."

"Doctors," groaned Casey. "You told him doctors saw me, in a hospital?"

"Well, yes," his mother said again. "But he isn't coming home and he's only phoned four times since I got here."

"Only four times?" Casey groaned as his mother took the pillow from behind him and he eased himself down. "*Only* four times?"

Alone again, Casey grinned as he thought of his dad's remarks as he left for Ottawa.

"You know, Casey, when I retired from the RCMP I sort of imagined a lot of rest and relaxation, but with you stumbling across mysteries right and left, there seem to be as many bad guys in my life as there ever were."

"Well, like you always say, Dad, 'an idle mind is a dull mind' — I'm just trying to keep you sharp."

"Okay, okay, Casey," his father had said, "but in future would you just pick me up a book of crossword puzzles?"

"Dad'll be glad to learn I'm not involved in any more manhunts," Casey said aloud before yawning and going back to sleep.

In the middle of the night, Casey saw something that made it impossible for him to go back to sleep: his mother's shadow against the wall of his room as she stopped by his bed. How could he have forgotten it — the shadow of the one-legged man in the room next to his closet at the Hoodoo Hotel? And the face of the man closing the drapes? And the conversation about the planned robbery of the museum? He should have remembered sooner. He had to talk to Dr. Norman right away. He checked his watch: 3 a.m. Too early.

Casey went over in his mind what he'd heard. He figured he'd better put it in point form, the way his dad always insisted on, and he'd better write it down. He turned on the bedside light and looked around for something to write with and write on. Nothing. His backpack was in the closet across the room; he had a pencil and a notebook in it.

Walking slowly to the closet was no problem, but when Casey stooped to pick up his pack from the floor, his head began to spin. He eased down to the floor, got the notebook and pencil out of his pack, closed the closet door, and shuffled back to bed.

How had the conversation started? He remembered now that there'd been two conversations.

Point 1. Late on the night of Thursday, June 17, I got up to close the window of my room at the Hoodoo Hotel, Drumheller, Alberta (which was the closet-room adjoining Room 327) because the smell of garbage was so powerful, and heard two men in conversation in the next room, whose open window was at right angles to mine.

Point 2. They were discussing the fact that they had spent a lot of time that day in one special area of the Tyrrell Museum paying particular attention to the artifacts on display there, stuff that one of them had photographed with a small, hidden video camera while the other distracted the guard by falling down.

Point 3. The purpose of these activities was so that they could make a report of their findings to "The Man" somewhere in the United States. "The Man" was to let them know which of the artifacts they had photographed they were to come back and steal.

Point 4. One man said he'd told some security guards from the Tyrrell he was getting a job there and they'd told him that the area he asked about had its own entrance and security system.

That was the first conversation. Did he really have to tell Dr. Norman about throwing up and dropping his hat in the dumpster? No. He'd just say … Casey felt very tired. He lay back against the pillows and closed his eyes. But he willed himself not to go to sleep. He figured he'd better carry on while the memory of the conversation was still fresh in his mind. What was to say he wouldn't forget it by morning like he'd forgotten it before?

Point 5. I saw the shadow of one man: He had only one leg. I saw the face of the other man.

Point 6. …

# CHAPTER FIVE

"Casey? Wake up Casey."

Casey opened his eyes. Dr. Norman was shaking him gently by the shoulder.

"Your mother called me when she read your notes. Feel up to explaining them for me?"

"Sure, Dr. Norman." Casey sat up and yawned mightily. "I wrote down pretty well all I remembered…."

"Well," Dr. Norman handed Casey his notes, "you didn't finish what you were writing under 'Point 6.'"

Casey looked at the list. He tried to think what "Point 6" was going to be about. He couldn't and handed back the paper, saying, "If there was more to say, I don't remember what it could have been."

"Well, if you do remember anything else be sure to tell me."

Dr. Norman sat down on the chair beside Casey's bed. A large jug of lemonade was on the bedside table. Casey shook his head when Dr. Norman offered to pour him a glass.

"I'm going to tell you what steps have already been taken in light of your report, Casey, and then I have a huge favour to ask of you on behalf of the Tyrrell. The first step, of course, is that the museum's alarm system is being revamped to frustrate the kind of disarming your 'friends' were going to try." He poured himself a glass of lemonade and went on.

"The RCMP have checked at the Hoodoo Hotel for information about the two men in the room next to yours. The Regina address the men had given at the registration desk was false, so doubtless the names they gave were false as well. Certainly there is no indication anywhere that they were from the United States. The licence plate number tallied with one stolen from a car in Lethbridge last week. A guard at the museum remembered the incident of a man falling. He didn't realize the man had an artificial leg, though; he just remembered that he limped a little."

"All this has got done since I went to sleep?" Casey asked.

"Well, it's about four hours since your mother brought me your notes, and museum security and the RCMP got onto it right away." Dr. Norman took a swallow of lemonade and added, "I'm expecting to hear any minute about another step we're taking … and, by the way, Casey, I must say you really know how to write a report."

"Yeah, well, Dad likes reports 'crystal clear.'"

Casey was hoping Dr. Norman would tell his dad how good the report was: maybe he'd not get such heck for the sunburn.

"Dr. Norman, I'm really glad my report has been a help. I have to admit, though, I find all of this a little weird.... I mean, why would robbers and some guy from the States be so interested in the fossils in the museum? Dinosaurs are popular, I know, but I don't really understand why they'd come all the way here to steal some."

"Casey, do you know of the importance of this area in the realm of international palaeontology?"

"Well." Casey thought a minute. "Mr. Deverell's given us a whole series of pre-trip lectures. I know different sorts of exploration between Brooks and Drumheller have been going on for over a century. And I know George Dawson first came in 18 ... was it 1874?"

"Right." Dr. Norman nodded. "He found bones along the Milk River. Joseph Burr Tyrrell came in 1884, ten years later. He accidentally came across the first skull found of an *Albertosauros*. Then came Weston."

"I've heard of Weston," Casey said. "Wasn't he the first guy to boat down the Red Deer looking for beds of bones?"

"He was," said Dr. Norman. "In the 1890s he floated south on the Red Deer, from north of Drumheller to where Dinosaur Provincial Park is today."

"And the *Lambeosaurus*," Casey said. "It was named after somebody, Lambe."

"Lawrence Lambe, a palaeontologist who came after Weston."

"Then came that Mr. Brown." Casey was pleased to remember. "Barnum Brown, from the American Museum of Natural History in New York."

Dr. Norman's cellphone rang and he nodded to Casey as he answered it.

"Yes. Yes. That's right. Okay. Ask him." He closed his phone. "Where were we?"

"Barnum Brown," said Casey.

"Right. Here's his story. Well, he was working for a time in Montana and came up in 1909. He found thousands and thousands of specimens. For years he shipped as many as four boxcars of bones back to the United States every summer for reconstruction in American museums."

"How come he could do that?" Casey asked. "Take all 'our' bones?"

"No laws to prevent it," Dr. Norman told him. "But the Geological Survey of Canada got wise and hired Charles H. Sternberg from Kansas to make a record of what the whole area held. Sternberg did some collecting for Canadian museums, but his focus was more on locating and siting the richer bonebeds."

"Mr. Deverell told us palaeontologists still use Sternberg's photos and geographical notes to re-explore sites he didn't have time to fully dig."

"Right again," Dr. Norman looked impressed.

He poured himself more lemonade, and this time Casey asked for a glass as well and took a cookie from a plate within his reach.

Dr. Norman continued. "You can appreciate what an immense and wonderful variety of fossils there are in Alberta, and that brings us back to the theft problem. Twenty years ago, there wasn't all that much interest in fossils; the fossil world was small. Now, fossils of every sort, but especially dinosaur fossils, are in hot demand."

"I'll bet old Barney played a part in their being popular," Casey suggested.

"Some people think he did." Dr. Norman smiled. "Some say it started with Michael Crichton's book *Jurassic Park* and the movie made from it. However it was sparked, it's a huge, unstoppable, worldwide mania, with private collectors playing the biggest part."

"So, how come the governments just can't say, 'All the fossils are for everybody'?"

"Oh, it's a real can of worms." Dr. Norman poured out the last of the lemonade. "In the States, there's a real battle going on. The amateur collectors are getting all sorts of support in their demands for their constitutional right to search any land, public or private, and to take and sell just about anything; and the scientists are trying to study and preserve important specimens."

"Sounds like the same kind of fights they had down there over government forests." Casey frowned. How do I know that, he wondered? Then it came to him. "I know how I know that," he said. "My grandma is a great Gene Autrey fan — she's got every film he ever made, and her favourite is *Riders of the Whistling Pines* — it's got to be fifty years old and I've seen it four times. The villains in it are destroying all the timber on a government forest preserve and the good guys are trying to stop them."

"Same sort of battle, but while you can plant more trees you can't grow more dinosaurs," Dr. Norman observed. "Palaeontologists just hate the thought of significant fossils disappearing into somebody's living room." He added, "Museums and academic institutions want to keep them for the public at large. But people do steal from museums as well as from public lands. A few years ago a *Tyrannosaurus* jaw disappeared from a big museum. Sometime later, it turned up after passing through the hands of a dealer in Germany."

"Are things like that jaw worth a lot?" Casey wanted to know.

"Every sort of fossil you can think of is sold all over the place: on the web; at auctions; and through what's called the black market. There, a single *T. rex* tooth can bring $20,000 U.S."

"Black market. I've read about that," Casey said.

"Yes. A market where things are sold illegally. With such big money at stake, current laws on both sides of the Canada–U.S. border haven't been enough to curb smuggling, except out of Alberta."

"What's different about us?" Casey asked.

Dr. Norman's cell rang again. "Yes," he said. "He'll do it?" After a long pause he repeated, "He'll do it? Good." He closed his phone.

"I'll be back in a few minutes, Casey. We'll finish our talk later. In the meantime, try to remember anything else you can tell us."

Casey lay back on his pillows, wondering what the heck was going on. He tried, but couldn't think of anything about the planned robbery apart from what he'd already reported.

In less than five minutes Dr. Norman was back in Casey's room.

"I'll fill you in about what's going on later, Casey." Dr. Norman sat down again. "Where were we?" he asked.

"You were about to tell me how come it's only in Alberta that it's against the law to remove fossils," Casey told him.

Dr. Norman nodded. "Right. Well, here our Historical Resources Act makes clear that 'all fossil material whether on public or private lands belongs to the public trust.'"

"What happens in the rest of Canada and in the U.S.?" Casey wondered. He was getting tired again, but he wanted to know.

"In the United States, all fossils on public land belong to the American people, but collectors often ignore the law. Many times, agents have found holes as big as ten feet deep dug on public land, and there are reports of flatbed trucks seen, again on public land, carting off huge amounts of valuable fossils. In most of Canada, fossils are formally protected only in national parks. In both countries, fossils on private land belong to the landowners, except again for Alberta, and in the last while, Nova Scotia."

"Pretty complicated." Casey tried not to yawn.

"It gets more complicated," Dr. Norman said, "because, while collecting vertebrate fossils on public land is strictly forbidden in Alberta, authorized scientists may excavate and study fossils under permit from the Tyrrell. On private lands, only surface-collected vertebrate fossils may be kept, but these must be photographed and registered with the Tyrrell and can't be removed from the province."

"Pretty strict," said Casey.

"But not perfect." Dr. Norman shook his head. "Anyway, whether your men are trying to steal for a private collector or for a dealer, we've got to stop them."

"We?" asked Casey. "Like in the museum and me?"

"Exactly," Dr. Norman replied. "Now, here comes the favour: Since you're the only person who can identify the two men in question, and since we've no idea when they might be back to steal the artifacts, the Tyrrell would like to hire you for the summer to keep an eye out for them. You can stay with us. Mandy will be back here next week but we've another room we've been planning to make into a guest room."

"I'll have to ask Mom and Dad," Casey said, "but I think it would be great!"

"Your mother has already been in touch with Ottawa, and they're tracking down your father. She says it would be fine with her and should be okay with him. Apparently, they're planning some big renovations on your house, and think it would be easier on everybody if you weren't there. We should have the word from your dad by this evening."

"If it's all right with Dad, when would I start?" Casey wanted to know.

"Well, you've only one week more of school, right?"

"Right." Casey nodded. "Exam week."

"How about coming the Monday after. In the meantime, we're going to have Trevor Treadwell, who manages our Museum Gift and Souvenir Shop, take over the table where you will be sitting and watching. He'll have a description of the men and will report anything suspicious. His helper will run the gift shop for that week, and Trevor will be handy if any questions about the shop come up. Now, back to you. I'm not sure yet what your job description will be, but you'll be paid double the minimum wage; you'll be doing cataloguing work for us as well as watching." Dr. Norman stood up. He turned as he headed for the door and said, "everyone is so grateful for your information."

"That's okay." Casey waved as Dr. Norman went out and closed Casey's door.

"Okay? It's great!" Casey whispered to himself. He got out another piece of paper and started writing down all the things he was going to spend his money on.

*A new wide-brimmed hat*

*A* … he was fast asleep.

# CHAPTER SIX

On his last afternoon in Drumheller, Dr. Norman showed Casey where in the foyer of the Tyrrell he would he stationed.

"That'll be your desk and chair right in front of that pillar," Dr. Norman said, pointing to a long table facing the entry doors. Sitting at the table in a rotating wooden office chair was a skinny man with short-cropped, mouse-brown hair and dark-rimmed glasses.

As they stood for a minute for Casey to take in the scene, Dr. Norman told him, "You'll have trays of rocks and pieces of bone to measure and classify to the best of your ability — always remember to double-check your measurements — the classifications will be rechecked by our staff."

"Now," he said, "come and meet Trevor."

"Incidentally," he added, "we're not planning to tell Trevor all the details of what's really going down: He understands who he's to look for and has been told you will be taking over when you're free to come." He paused a few seconds, and continued in a low voice, "I have to warn you, though, Trevor is jealous of anyone horning in on 'his' territory."

"I won't be, will I?" Casey asked.

"No. He has his own job in the gift shop and you'll have nothing to do with that. We'll be telling him you've been hired as a sort of palaeotology intern for the summer; as well, he knows you're supposed to look out for the men in question. He knows you're the one who's seen them."

They passed the Gift Shop along a wall next to the main exit and walked toward "Casey's" table. Trevor was sitting with his arms folded and a belligerent look on his face. Casey guessed the guy was in his mid-twenties.

"Trevor," Dr. Norman began, "I'd like you to meet Casey Templeton." Casey shot out his hand. Trevor didn't. "Casey," Dr. Norman continued, "who, as you know, saw the men in question. He has a great interest in palaeontology as well and is going to be a Tyrrell intern for the summer."

Trevor grunted.

"Casey will be taking over the surveillance job you're doing now when he's free in about a week. He'll also be sorting and categorizing stones and bone fragments as well. Eventually, the stones will land up for sale in your shop."

"The Tyrrell doesn't have interns," Trevor complained.

"It does now," Dr. Norman told him, "and I want you to show every courtesy to Casey."

A customer walked into the shop. Trevor glanced over to see that a clerk was helping her. He grunted again. (Casey thought, *Never heard anyone grunt like that*.) When Trevor saw the customer was attended to, he sneered at Casey and lowered his head.

Dr. Norman raised his eyebrows in a "see what I mean" expression and he and Casey walked over to stand near the door.

"Okay. So I sit over there facing the door, and ...?" Casey began.

"We'll have the procedure worked out for you by the time you get back here."

Dr. Norman pointed above the door and Casey looked up.

"That's a surveillance camera, Casey, and there's one above where you'll be sitting, so the museum will have photos of everyone who enters.... It's just that no one but you really knows what these men look and sound like."

As they walked out the door, Casey told Dr. Norman about a couple of ideas he'd had related to his watching job. Dr. Norman was impressed and said, "Good thinking, Casey."

They walked in silence for a couple of minutes, then Dr. Norman asked, "You'll be starting a week from next Monday, so you'll be coming down on the Sunday?"

Casey nodded.

"Tell your parents they're invited for an early supper."

"Thanks so much" — Casey smiled up at him — "I'm sure my dad will be back by then and I know he'd like it a lot if he could check out my set-up here."

"Well, I've got some letters to write," said Dr. Norman, looking at his watch. "I'll see you later."

Casey walked back to the Normans', got all his gear together, had a good supper, and went to bed early so he'd not have any trouble getting up to catch the 6:45 a.m. bus to Richford.

He got up as soon as his alarm rang, dressed quietly, and went down to the Normans' kitchen.

He drank juice from the fridge and ate the cereal and muffins Mrs. Norman had left for him on the kitchen table.

"A note," Casey said out loud. "I should leave a note."

On a sheet torn from his notebook, Casey wrote:

> *Thank you both so very much for taking such good care of me.*
>
> *I will do my very best to help you catch the men who are planning to rob the Tyrrell. See you in ten days.*
>
> *Casey.*

He put the note in the middle of the kitchen table. Then, with his backpack in place on his now healing back, he walked out the back door and down to the Drumheller bus depot.

# CHAPTER SEVEN

"So, Casey," Mike said as they walked down the school corridor toward their lockers, "how could you concentrate on a Math test when you've got all this summer business on your mind?"

"Easy," Casey said. "Either I do well in all my exams or there's no way my dad will let me take on that Tyrrell job. He'll be home Saturday and will want a report on how I did."

"You won't have your results by then," Mike said.

"No," Casey agreed, "but I'll have a good idea of how the tests went."

"We'll really miss you on the baseball team — you are one strong catcher."

"I've been using one of those hard rubber hand things you squeeze over and over. It's a great way to build your arm and hand muscles. Here, shake a paw."

Mike grasped Casey's hand and Casey squeezed hard.

"Yeow!" Mike shouted. "Let go!"

"See?" said Casey.

"See nothing, I feel," Mike said, massaging his right hand with his left. "That's a wicked grip you've got."

"Yeah, and it's going to get a lot wickeder over the summer. That's something I work on when I'm watching TV."

"I'm going to get me one of those squeeze things, so you watch out — by the end of the summer we'll see who's strongest."

Mike's locker door slammed as he said, "You hear about the party old prissy pants, Greta Maitland, is giving Friday night?" he asked. "We're all invited to her family's big house for supper and a dance. I can just see it. The girls will likely have to wear little white gloves and we'll be expected to wear shirts and ties."

"You have got to be kidding!" Casey was appalled. "Did they really say that's what we have to wear?"

"Well, no," Mike admitted. "But can't you just imagine it?"

"All we have to do is make sure nobody wears a shirt and tie. There's no way the Maitlands are going to kick out all the boys. Greta wouldn't allow it — she likes boys too much."

"I haven't said that I was going to go yet," said Mike. "Can't we have some sort of year-end celebration of our own?"

"Okay by me. I don't think I've been invited anyway," Casey said.

"Yes you have," Mike told him. "Greta got up in home room and invited the whole class."

"But maybe nobody told me," Casey said hopefully. "How about we head out to the Old Willson With Two L's Place and party?"

"You been out there since that hate gang was turfed?" Mike wondered.

"No," Casey said. "Have you?"

"No," said Mike. "My folks heard about what went on there last fall and put it off limits."

"Mine too," said Casey. "But they wouldn't have to know. We could take out a bunch of stuff to eat and an iPod and some wood for a fire. It'd beat the heck out of a party at the Maitlands'."

"Who else will we ask?" Mike was warming up to the idea.

"Any guys who haven't told Greta they'd be there," Casey said. "We'll ask around, subtle like. Not tell the others what we have in mind until we know they're free."

By Thursday they knew. Every other boy in the class had told Greta they'd be at her party.

"Still want to go to the Willson place if it's just the two of us?" asked Mike.

"I do if you do," Casey said. "I'll bring my new iPod. And I'll bring a litre of Coke and some chips and a dip."

"I've got two albums you haven't heard, and I'll bring doughnuts," said Mike.

"We'll need wood for the fire." Casey was remembering how he'd burned up everything he could find in the house trying to keep Mr. Deverell and himself warm the night he went there last fall.

"I got wood," said Mike.

"Sounds good." Casey figured it could be fun. "Now all we have to do is get that English exam over tomorrow afternoon and — CELEBRATION TIME!"

***

"Mom," said Casey as he headed out the back door, "I don't know how late I'll be."

"Be home fifteen minutes after Greta's party's over. You know your father's rules," his mother said. Casey winced. His mother just assumed he was going to Greta's, and he hadn't told her the truth.

"But Dad's not here," Casey told her. "What say you set some new rules — just for tonight?"

"Sure." His mother smiled. "Be home twenty minutes after the party's over."

"Oh, Mom." Casey hitched on his backpack. He knew his mother wouldn't question him about the backpack; he never went anywhere without it.

"You don't have to wait up," he said from the open door.

"I'll wait up," his mother replied. "Have fun."

Casey and Mike didn't talk much as they crossed the field to the Old Willson With Two L's Place. *Was Mike thinking the same thing he was?* wondered Casey. *That this might not be the single smartest thing they were doing?* But the night was warm and the sky was still light and it would be fun to see the old place again.

"You bring any matches for the fire?" Mike asked.

"No," said Casey. "Didn't you?"

"No." Mike stopped. "A lotta good this wood I'm carrying's going to do. Shall I pitch it?"

"Maybe there'll be matches there," Casey said, but he didn't believe it. "Maybe other people have been using the old place like we used to before...."

"Yeah, before those Hate Cell guys almost finished off old Deverell and you both almost froze to death. I've heard. I've heard."

"Well, don't remind me." Casey did not want to remember the last time he'd hiked across this field to the old house and found Mr. Deverell unconscious, almost covered by snow, and with a huge gash in his head.

"You did bring a flashlight?" Mike asked.

"Sure," Casey reassured him. "If we can't have a fire, we can prop the flashlight in the fireplace. It'll be better, really. We won't have to worry about sparks flying around."

"Sure no signs of life out here," Mike said as they climbed the sagging fence round the Willson property when they found the high gate locked. "We'll have a great time on our own."

"Sure." But Casey was anything but sure. They were near the house now. The evening sun should have been reflecting from the windows. There was no reflection.

"The windows are boarded up," Casey said.

"Hope the door isn't," Mike said as they turned the corner of the house.

"No boards," Casey said, not sure if this was good or bad. "Maybe it's locked." He led the way up the front steps and tried the door handle. The door swung inward and as it did a siren wailed louder and louder and louder.

"Ohmygosh," Casey yelled, "let's get the heck out of here!"

They did. They fairly flew across the field back to the edge of town, their backpacks thumping, their hearts pounding.

When they could talk again, Mike stopped, dropped the wood from his backpack in a heap and asked, "What now?"

Casey thought a minute.

"Now we go to Greta Maitland's fancy end-of-school-year party."

"We do?" asked Mike. "We never said we'd come."

"We never said we wouldn't," Casey replied. "Nobody's going to care if we show up."

# CHAPTER EIGHT

The bright lights on the Maitlands' front porch looked welcoming, but all the curtains were drawn.

"I can't hear any music." Mike stood listening. "Can you?"

"No," Casey said, ringing the doorbell. "They're probably still eating. I sure hope so," he added, "and I sure hope there's some left for us."

The door opened wide and Greta's father, in a pair of very tight jeans and a red-checked flannel shirt, turned back into the hall and shouted, "Hey, Greta, your lost sheep have arrived!"

"Come in, boys," he said softly, ushering them inside. "Am I glad to see you! Greta went upstairs in a sulk; couldn't believe anyone would refuse to come to her party. I swear she was ready to send everyone home."

"So," Greta said reprovingly, as she stood on the stair landing, "you finally deigned to come to the party I've been working on for weeks. Well, Dad and I." She sounded mad, but Casey could tell she was very relieved to see him and Mike.

"Sorry we're late." Mike was looking around. "Where IS the party? It's quiet as a morgue."

"Everyone's in our video theatre; it's sound proof," Mr. Maitland said, not in a boastful way like Greta would have said it. "Greta, take your guests' packs and show them down."

Ungraciously, Greta reached for Mike's pack.

"Smells like doughnuts — didn't you think there'd be enough food here?" She hung Mike's pack in a large hall closet; taking Casey's, she noticed the neck of a big bottle of Coke sticking out. "And you brought your own drink? I have to think neither one of you has ever been to a real party. Come on."

Nobody even turned around as Greta slid open a pocket door and motioned Casey and Mike to some empty seats. She sat beside Casey and whispered, "It's *Friday the Thirteenth*."

"Yeah, I know," Casey whispered back. "Great!"

He looked around the miniature movie theatre with its huge screen, and real semi-reclining theatre seats with arm recesses holding cartons full of popcorn. The sound was fantastic.

In a tense, silent part of the film, the sound of the sliding door being pushed open brought all heads around.

"Bryan!" Greta shouted, almost falling as she hurried back to get him. Greta led Bryan to a seat beside her. She sat there watching Bryan instead of the movie.

"Ah ha!" Casey said to himself. "I'll bet Greta's going to be in a much better mood now."

She was. Her face glowed with happiness and she left Bryan's side only when the film was over and her father called her to cut the huge cake on the dining-room table.

Interested to hear how Bryan had got along at his new school, Casey said, "I've missed you, Bryan. How did it go down east?"

"Fine," Bryan said. "Really good. And the best part is I'm back on the Internet."

"But you've been banned from using the net for two years."

"Oh heck," Bryan said. "That was here. Down there, the school has computers everywhere you look and who's going to know I'm online?"

"I think you're taking a big chance." Casey looked troubled. "Outside your parents, the police, and the lawyers, only my mother and I know about your Internet hate connections and the trouble they got you into. I can't believe you'd take a chance on getting caught." He shook his head and went on, "I'll bet the school knows you're forbidden to use the net. They're not dumb. Someone's going to be snooping around and if you do get caught … well, I don't know exactly what will happen to you, but it ain't going to be good."

"Enough with the lecture, Casey," Bryan said, "with my father's connections, I can't see me getting into serious trouble. Besides, I'm not into that stuff anymore anyway, so forget I told you and don't squeal on me to your father. And don't play the heavy with me just because your dad beat mine in the mayor's race."

He walked away toward Greta, who was saving the first piece of cake she'd cut for him — a corner piece with lots of icing.

Casey shook his head sadly. *Bryan's starting to sound just like his father, and that's a bad sign*, he thought as he joined a group around the table.

"Nice to see you, Marcia," he said. He meant it. He didn't have a crush on Marcia any more, and besides, she and Terry were an item, but he still liked her. "Hi, Terry. Kevin."

"Heard about your summer job," Terry said. "We were hoping you'd be around for baseball and hockey camp."

"I was hoping so, too," said Casey. And he was. Richford was famous for its hockey winter and summer, and its summer hockey camp was the best in the province. He loved baseball too, and was looking forward to being the team's first-string catcher. "The job at the Tyrrell could end any day, so I might be back really soon."

"Try to be back for the mid-August barbecue," said Marcia. "If you thought last year's Halloween party was cool, you'll be amazed at this party. And as mayor, your dad'll be front and centre."

"I'll sure try to be there," Casey assured her.

***

"What a party!" Mike sighed. They'd thanked Greta and Mr. Maitland and started home.

"The movie was great, the food was wonderful, the music was sensational," Casey agreed. "And Greta may be a pain in the butt, but her old man sure knows how to throw a party."

"You figure he did most of it?" Mike asked.

"Look — Greta's mother's in Europe and Greta sure as heck didn't get all that food and have that room set up for dancing with all the blinking lights and buy all those good prizes. I'm telling you, Mr. Maitland did it all. He must love his daughter a lot, or …"

"Or he feels real sorry for her awful personality and is trying to make people like her in spite of herself."

"Whatever," said Casey. "I think we had an even better time there than we would have had on our own at the Old Willson Place."

"You figure?" Mike asked.

"I figure," Casey said, with conviction.

# CHAPTER NINE

"You'll need these."

Casey put the pile of clean underwear his mother handed him into his big duffle bag.

"I bought you some new socks, too," his mother continued. "I forgot them in the family room. I'll go get them; I'll be back in a couple of minutes."

He walked around his bed to where his father, who'd just got home, was standing, his outstretched hand holding a bright blue plastic folder about three inches square and a narrow dark blue one.

Casey knew what they were. He'd got the same ones yesterday when he'd opened an account at the Bank of Montreal in Richford, but there was no way he'd disappoint his dad by telling him.

Casey opened the blue folder and whistled. In the

"Balance" column, the total listed was $200.00. Yesterday, when he'd opened the account, the total in the Balance column was $12.00. He opened the cheque book. His name and address were printed on a set of plain, pale-green cheques. Yesterday, he'd ordered cheques with a cowboy in the background and his name and address printed on a saddle logo. Hoping his order for the cowboy cheques hadn't already been sent in, he said, "Thanks, Dad."

"I arranged your account from Ottawa. Can't be making money and not have a record of it," said Chief Superintendent Templeton. "I suggest you put every cent you make into your chequing account first, then draw out what cash you need."

"Sounds good," Casey agreed, "and I'll pay you back that $200."

"That's all right," said his father. "We'll be saving a lot more than that not having to feed you all summer. But you're going to have to pay the Normans for your room and board. It'll take a big whack out of what you make, but that's the way it's done."

Casey didn't think the Normans were going to make him pay for staying with them — after all, it'd been Dr. Norman's idea — but he said, "Right, Dad, I'll talk to the Normans."

"Any idea how much you'll be making?"

Casey went over to his desk, picked up a piece of paper and handed it to his father; it was a letter from Dr. Norman confirming the amount Casey would be paid.

"This came when you were away," he said.

"So you'll earn twice the Alberta minimum wage? Couldn't expect any more than that," his father said. "Know yet what the set-up of your observation post will be?"

"Yeah, it's pretty well finalized, but Dr. Norman wants

to talk the plan over with you when you and Mom drive me down to Drumheller tomorrow. But, basically, I'll be busy sizing small pieces of rock, including stones and semi-precious stones, for sale in the Museum Gift Shop, and categorizing bones and bone fragments at a table across the room from the entry turnstiles. Every time anyone comes in, a little light will come on at my table. I'll look directly at whoever is coming through the door and go back to my work until the light flashes again."

"Sounds like a well-thought-out plan," his dad said. "But how do you alert security?"

"I'll press a button that'll buzz in the security office," Casey told him, adding, "it was my idea about the light."

"Good thinking." His dad nodded. Then he said something else, which really surprised Casey. "We'll miss you."

He was out of the room before Casey could answer. Casey wondered if his dad would miss his company as well as his help in building the big house-addition that was in the works. Over the last year, they'd got to know each other. When Casey was growing up, his father had been gone from home most of the time, but they'd shared stuff in the last few months and a bond had begun to grow.

Casey paused in his packing, thinking about how he and his father had become real friends; there was still some distance, but he felt they'd come a long way.

Casey continued packing more stuff, mostly books, DVDs, his iPod, and a few computer games. He wondered how Mandy was doing. *Hope Mandy's going to be back soon — it'll sure be boring if she's not,* he thought. He'd learned that her throat had been so badly damaged that extra time was needed to build the muscle back up.

Casey sniffed. The wonderful smell of fresh-baked bread filled the air. Casey's stomach rumbled in reply.

"Gotta check this out," he muttered as he headed down the stairs. When he reached the bottom step he could hear his parents' voices in the kitchen.

"Any word on the attempted break-in at the Willson Place?" Casey's mother was asking.

"No," said his father, "but the Mounties did find a clear trail across the field from town to Willson's and from Willson's to town. And they do have a good set of fingerprints from the front door knob."

"Oh, no!" Casey whispered, trying frantically to remember if his fingerprints would be on file from the time Mr. Deverell was attacked. He didn't think they were, but he couldn't be completely sure. Would it be better if he confessed right now? Got it over with?

*Yes*, he decided, wondering as he went into the kitchen what kind of punishment his dad would dream up this time. At least, since it was summer, it wouldn't be snow shovelling, and he'd probably be at the Tyrrell for most of the grass-cutting season. Anyway, it wouldn't be mowing; his dad liked his riding mower too much to let anyone else use it. Maybe his father would say, "No problem, Casey, we'll just forget about it." Right.

"Dad," Casey, said hesitantly. "I might as well tell you; those fingerprints on the Willson door — they're mine."

As Casey went to sleep that night, he tried to remember just how many trees there were in their yard and in the neighbours' yards. Raking up all those leaves in the fall would sure cut into his social life. Oh well; it was still better than shovelling.

# CHAPTER TEN

The drive to Drumheller with his parents, and the supper at the Normans' worked out just fine. Casey's father said he couldn't think of anything that would improve the set-up for Casey in the Tyrrell's foyer.

The guest room the Normans had fitted up for Casey suited him a lot better than Mandy's fluffy bedroom. No, Mandy wasn't home yet, but her parents thought she would be back soon.

At first, Casey thought he'd landed a dream job. While the Tyrrell was open to the public from 9 a.m. to 9 p.m. every day in the summer, the administration had printed flyers that were given to everyone as they entered the building.

BECAUSE OF EXTENSIVE WORK BEING DONE
ON SOME OF THE SPECIMEN ROOMS, THE

FOLLOWING ROOMS WILL BE CLOSED AT 5
P.M. EVERY AFTERNOON. WE REGRET ANY
INCONVENIENCE THIS MAY CAUSE.

A list of rooms to be closed at 5 p.m. followed. The thinking was that the thieves would be interested only in the rooms they could carry items from, so wouldn't likely to be even entering the museum after five. Any researchers registered with the museum would have access to the otherwise-closed rooms.

Even with the shorter workday, Casey had to be on duty hours on end. He even ate the lunch Mrs. Norman made for him every day right at his post. The only problem was that the line-up at the turnstile had to be halted whenever Casey needed to go to the bathroom. He'd dash there and back so people at the turnstile didn't get too antsy. It seemed whenever he hurried to the men's room, however, Trevor was at the Museum Gift Shop door.

"What's the rush, oh chosen one," Trevor would hiss, "going to wet your pants?"

Casey ignored him as best he could, but it didn't make things any easier. As the eight-hour days stretched out, one after the other, he knew he sure was earning the double minimum wage he was being paid.

Going a different way back to the Normans', Casey spotted a poster in a store window advertising classes in kung fu.

The sign on the window started turning to CLOSED as Casey pushed open the door.

"Just a quick question," he said to a fit young man still holding the sign.

"Sure," the man said. "What can I do you for?"

Casey wasn't exactly sure what he wanted to ask.

"Ah," he said.

"Yeah?" asked the clerk.

"Well," Casey said slowly, "can someone who's fourteen sign up for kung fu?"

"Yes — the Junior Class is for fourteen- to sixteen-year-olds. But two things: the course started two weeks ago, and you'll need parental permission."

"Oh," Casey wasn't sure whether he was disappointed or not. "Well, is there some other exercise class I can take?" He was thinking of Mike getting stronger by the day.

"Well, our personal trainers can work one-on-one with a client. But it's pretty pricey." He walked over to a desk, the sign still in his hand, and took a paper from a file. "Here, this is a list of all our programs."

"Thanks a lot," said Casey, nodding as he opened the door and stepped out onto the sidewalk. He glanced back at the door: the sign was already turned to CLOSED.

Casey phoned his dad that night and talked over the idea of having a personal trainer. "It *is* expensive, Dad," he said. "I do go swimming some evenings and I use Mandy's Wii, but I sit around a lot too."

"Think about it a while longer," his father advised.

Casey hung up. "I'm going to go nuts if something doesn't happen soon," Casey told himself. After two weeks on the museum job, he called Mike in desperation.

"What's going on in Richford?" he asked. "I'll bet you guys are having a great time with hockey and baseball and just having fun."

"Yeah," Mike replied, "things are moving along."

"And here I am sitting for hours and hours every day as the crowds go by, and sitting for hours and hours every night on my own. Mandy hasn't come home yet and I am beyond bored."

"Well," Mike told him, "so far there's really not much going on up here besides sports. I have to tell you that the staff at the hockey school are terrific. Let's see — Greta Maitland broke her wrist showing off at a volleyball tourney. She'd demanded to be on a boys' team and fell backward when the ball she was reaching for whacked her hand."

"I'll bet she's blaming everyone in sight," Casey laughed. "What about the Willson investigation?" He hadn't told Mike about the fingerprint business.

"My dad says people think it was just mischief-makers and that the siren scared them off. He's heard the Mounties never even bothered to put a lock on the door. They figured that way out there people would get in if they wanted to — that a siren connected to the station would scare off any intruders."

"Sure worked for a couple of people we know, eh?" said Casey.

"I swear, Casey," Mike said, "I never moved so fast in my life. And that wood weighed a ton."

"So did the Coke and the other stuff," Casey said, wondering what else could they talk about.

"Boy," Mike said after a long pause, "are your folks ever making changes to your house. So help me, it's going to be as big as the Maitlands' place when they're done."

"You know, it's for a separate suite for my Grandma, and she's paying for it; she's not supposed to be totally on her own anymore."

"So that's what's going on," Mike said.

"My folks keep sending me pictures," Casey said. "You know, I'm going to get that lower level Dad and I built for Grandma's visits...."

"Whirlpool and all?" Mike asked.

"Whirlpool and all. Mom and Dad are making my present room into a TV room. I wish I could be there to watch all the changes, but this is the museum's busiest time and they're open every single day of the week."

"And you just sit there?" Mike said.

"Well, I do sit there nine to five, but when nobody's coming into the museum I keep busy measuring pieces of bones and rocks — I've sorted thousands of rocks and bones. I keep thinking I'll find more pieces of the tooth we found, but no luck.

"I even eat lunch right at my desk," Casey told him, "and when I have to go to the bathroom, I signal the guard and they find some reason to hold the line up for a few minutes.

"And still no luck spotting those two guys from the States." (He'd told Mike in strictest confidence what his job was and why he was the only one who could do it.) "I must have looked at a zillion faces and listened to a thousand voices and footsteps. Nothing."

They both were searching for something to say. Finally, Casey said, "There is one thing I have to tell you about. There's this guy named Trevor who manages the Gift Shop. He hates me because he thinks I've got this job he should have had — actually he had it for the week I wasn't here. I've seen him leaving my desk when I'm coming back from you-know-where, and I can tell he's been fiddling with 'my' rocks and bones."

"Fiddling, not taking, I hope," Mike asked.

"Not so far," Casey said, "but the rocks and stones I'm working on go for sale in the Museum Gift Shop, or wherever, and the bones and fragments are all ready to be labelled and checked, so anything he could get his hands on that's not catalogued he could sell on his own and not have to account for it."

"You better watch out," Mike warned him.

"I am," Casey assured him.

"So, what do you do all evening?" Mike wanted to know.

"I go for a swim for an hour at the 'Y' three nights a week, watch some TV — the Normans put one in my room, and I'm using Mandy's Wii a lot. Then I go to bed and read. The other four days, I walk around town a lot. So, I walk and read and play video games and watch more TV."

"What about Mandy? When is she coming home?"

"They say in a week. She's starting to do really well. Yeah, things should pick up when Mandy gets here. And Mike — one good thing. The Normans won't take any money for my room and board so I'm really socking it away."

"Lucky you," said Mike. "I'm lucky if I get five bucks an hour helping Dad."

"I'll be rich enough for both of us," Casey said. "When this is all over, let's talk our folks into a trip to Edmonton to 'do' West Edmonton Mall and see the Cracker Cats." Casey knew the one thing Mike liked better than CDs was baseball, and while it wasn't pro ball it was semi-pro and pretty darn good.

"You're on!" Mike hooted.

# CHAPTER ELEVEN

Twice Casey thought he spotted the men, and buzzed museum security. The first time, a man with a cane came through the turnstile and a few minutes later a man with shaggy eyebrows that almost joined entered the museum foyer. When Casey pointed out the second man, the guard smiled. "That's Dr. Foss, big-time palaeontologist from the University of Calgary."

"Oh, sorry," said Casey.

"Don't be," the guard told him. "Better to err on the side of caution."

The second time, Casey was sure. Two men came through the turnstile one right after the other. The second man, who again had eyebrows exactly like those of the man Casey had seen and heard in the Hoodoo Hotel, stepped forward and put his right hand under the elbow of the first man, who was limping. Casey pressed the security buzzer. He nodded toward the men as two security guards appeared.

One guard approached the men: the other stood beside Casey's table.

"It's a rather difficult walk up these ramps," Casey heard the first guard say to the two men. "We have wheelchairs available. Can I get you folks one?"

"That's mighty kind of you," the limping man said. "I broke my ankle a while ago and the darn thing still hurts a lot. You mind pushing me around, Bill?" he asked the other man.

"Not a bit, Wilf," replied his companion. "But you'll owe me big. One two-pound steak when we pass through Calgary tomorrow."

"You got it."

The first man eased himself into the wheelchair the guard had rolled up.

"Got a long drive ahead of you tomorrow, I take it," Casey heard the guard ask.

"Nah," said the seated man, "just to Cochrane. We run the garage across from the big ice-cream stand — get a lot of business from all the Calgarians who drive over there on weekends for ice cream."

"That right?" said the guard. "I'll have to drive down one of these days."

"If you do, come see us," Bill said, as he pushed the wheelchair along. "Our garage is called 'The Brothers'; we'll top off your tank for free."

Casey reached down for his backpack; the oh-so-frustrating and humiliating day over at last. "Wouldn't you know," he said to himself, "The darn thing's caught under my chair leg." He got down on his hands and knees to unwind the strap. When it was freed Casey stood up. There was a long white envelope on his desk. *They've fired me*, he thought. *I've wasted everyone's time and the museum's money, and they've fired me.*

Sighing, he opened the middle drawer of his small desk and took out a letter opener. He could hear his father's voice saying, "Never rip open an envelope; you might tear what's inside or you might make it harder to read a mailing date or a name."

Casey dutifully slid the edge of the letter opener under the flap, slit open the envelope, took out the paper inside, looked at it, and gasped.

Not a dismissal notice. It was a cheque. A cheque for his first month's duties. A big cheque. Casey sat at the desk and laid the cheque on it. He saw Trevor sliding towards him and just got the cheque turned over in time.

"Stashing away your ill-gotten gains, I see," Trevor made a lunge for the cheque but Casey caught his wrist and gave it a hard twist.

"Mind your own business, Trevor," Casey said as he pocketed his cheque.

"If you're getting more than me for just sitting around, I'm going to make an official complaint."

"And if you don't stop bugging me, I'm going to make a complaint."

Trevor slunk off and Casey sat down.

"My money," he whispered, no longer tired or bored or frustrated or humiliated: just happy. "I earned this. It's all mine."

He sat staring at the cheque. "Maybe I won't cash it. Maybe I'll frame it and look at it. Then again …" Into his mind flashed the imagine of a mountain bike he'd seen on the last walk he'd taken into downtown Drumheller. It was a flame red. It had all the bells and whistles. It had more gears than he'd ever seen. *And*, Casey thought to himself as he picked up the cheque and smiled a huge smile, *I can afford it!*

# CHAPTER TWELVE

"It'll be light for hours," Mandy said. She and Casey were sitting on the Normans' veranda. Mandy was eating Jell-O and Casey was enjoying a chocolate sundae. He looked over at Mandy.

"Is that all the dessert you're going to have?"

"Well, I have to eat things that won't irritate my throat, and with this darn milk allergy of mine, I can't have ice cream or puddings or anything like that."

"When are you going to be able to eat some more solid food?" Casey asked. "I make a heck of an omelette."

"Somehow I can't see you cooking, Casey. But when I can eat an omelette, I'll let you know."

"Good," said Casey.

Mandy was pretty well; she looked better every day, and the wonderful glow she'd had the day Casey'd seen her in the cafeteria was slowly coming back. But she still wasn't supposed to speak loudly or do any jumping or heavy lifting — or swimming.

When she'd first come home things had been awkward, Mandy not being used to anyone but her family living there. Mandy had not been her usual friendly self and couldn't hide her resentment when Casey went off swimming. Casey finally realized it really got to Mandy that she couldn't practise too, and cut his pool visits to one a week instead of three. Mandy was grateful and the good times started.

"I am so glad you're back in town, Mandy," Casey told her, thinking how easy she was to be with and, having grown up in a family of four boys, how different it was spending so much time with a girl — especially this girl. "It's great to have something to look forward to after work. My days are awfully boring."

Mandy put down her empty dish and smiled. "Your days are boring? Try mine."

The Normans had had a celebration dinner for Mandy when she got home a couple of weeks ago. She could have only soup and Jell-O, but she didn't seem to mind.

"It is so great to be back," she sighed contentedly. "All those weeks away with only reading and TV. You'll be happy to know, dear parents," she continued, "I've finished all the homework for the rest of the year in social studies, so, when I finally get back to school, I can start a senior biology course."

Mrs. Norman smiled. "Had a hunch you'd not be wasting your time." Mandy attended St. Hilda's, an exclusive, academically challenging girls-only school in Calgary.

"You planned anything for us to do tonight?" Casey wondered.

"Dad's going to take us to Horsethief Canyon as soon as he can get away from the museum."

"That's great. I've been looking forward to seeing it."

Whenever Casey was free, he and Mandy would set off on an adventure. They'd bicycle north on the west bank of the Red Deer River, cross at Bleriot Ferry, the little motor–and–winch contraption said to be the busiest ferry in Alberta, and ride home along the east bank. Mandy's bike was good, but the red one Casey'd bought with his first cheque was much better. It could do about anything. He loved that bike. Some nights he even dreamed about it.

When they weren't riding, they'd hitch rides with some of the museum staff — once south to the hoodoos to spend a couple of hours exploring among the odd mushroom-like sandstone formations sculptured over the centuries by wind and water erosion.

Another time they went on part of a *Centrosaurus* bonebed hike in Dinosaur Provincial Park, one of the world's largest dinosaur fields. Their guide on that trip said palaeontologists learned an enormous amount about the behaviour and lifestyle of dinosaurs from beds such as these.

"The whole place looks so uninhabited." Sitting in the shade of a sandstone overhang, Mandy shivered. "You'd think there wouldn't be any wildlife around here, but look." She pointed to a mule deer finding what coolness it could in a coulee.

"And there's a scorpion right by your boot." Casey pointed.

Mandy quickly moved her foot.

"Better that than a rattlesnake, at least," Mandy said. A comfortable silence surrounded them as the guide took the rest of the group further along the trail. "I'd like to go to Horseshoe Canyon again one of these days — it's farther away than Horsethief where Dad'll be driving us tonight. And I'd like to go to the LITTLE church they say 'seats ten thousand people, six at a time.' Want to come?"

"Sure," Casey said, "I've never seen either one."

"Horsethief Canyon's not open to the public at night," Mandy explained, "but Dad says we can wander around the top of it while he has his meeting."

"All right!" Casey gazed into space thinking maybe this time he'd find all the parts of a dinosaur tooth, or even a whole tooth, or …

Mandy could read his mind. "A lot of people explore that site every day, so don't get your hopes up on making a big find."

The view from the top of Horsethief Canyon was spectacular. They'd brought a couple of folding chairs and were comfortably taking in the sights. As with everywhere along the river valley, the walls of the canyon were earth tones of every variety: black, brown, ochre, tan.

"Look at all those gullies and slashes," Casey swept his hand from side to side. "I read that a horse thief could drag a horse into one of them and hide forever in that maze."

"Easy to believe," Mandy said. "Let's walk a little way down there."

"Are you sure you'll be okay?"

"We'll just take an easy hike," Mandy said.

"How much time do we have before your dad picks us up?" Casey asked.

Mandy checked her watch. "About two hours," she told him. "It'll stay light at least that long."

"Up here, maybe," Casey observed, "not in the valley."

Casey climbed down toward a shadowy area that looked like a cave's mouth.

"That cave looks pretty near," he called back. "Let's give it a look."

"It's almost too near," Mandy said as she caught up with Casey. "And it's only about four feet deep. I checked it out last time I was here and so has every other visitor to Horsethief Canyon."

"Oh." Casey looked around. He pointed toward a far hill. "Then let's go across to that narrow valley between those hills."

"Where?" Mandy asked him. Casey pointed again. "Yeah, I see it. I never even noticed it when I was here before; let's go."

After walking for half an hour they didn't seem to be getting any closer to the far hill, but they were deep in the valley. The evening air began to have a hint of chill. As Mandy started to walk more quickly, her boot hit a rock and she fell forward. Casey knelt beside her. Realizing what such a jar could do to her fragile throat, he said with concern, "You okay, Mandy?"

"I don't feel great." Her voice sounded raspy. "My throat is starting to sting. The doctors said if that happened, I was to stay still and take my pain pills."

"You have them with you?" asked Casey.

"Yeah," said Mandy, taking a small packet from the back pocket of her shorts.

"So lie down," Casey said, his brain racing. "Here, put my jacket under you and huddle into yours. I'll climb up and wait for your dad. He can call for help on his cellphone."

"But it'll be totally dark down here by then." Mandy's faint whisper could hardly be heard. She spread Casey's jacket onto the cold clay and eased herself down. "How'll they find me? These pills are very strong and make me so sleepy I'll probably be out of it. I won't hear people calling, and I'm not supposed to shout."

"Right," Casey said. "You don't have any matches, do you?" he asked hopefully.

"No."

"Okay, so we can't make a fire even if there was any wood," Casey said. "Here's what we'll do. Your dad's bound to have some sort of light in the Jeep. I'll take it, find you again — I'm sure I can, then I'll signal with the light when he comes with help. You get as comfortable as you can. I'll be back."

It was twilight in the valley now, and the air was definitely cool. Casey looked toward the summit of Horsethief Canyon. The sky beyond the summit still looked light and almost without colour.

Casey figured he could get up there before the valley got totally dark, and started the climb. The rough, red-clay canyon walls were almost black now and the deep slashes in their surface made climbing difficult. He turned to check on Mandy's location and could barely see the humped outline of his friend.

*How will I find her once it's really dark*? Casey wondered. I'll need some sort of marker. Casey looked round. A jet-black area far to his right told him he was level with the mouth of the cave all the visitors went to. He felt around for a rock, then took off his T-shirt, spread it fully out, and put the rock on it.

*That'll hold it down*, he thought.

Now he was really chilly and scrambled up as fast as the uneven canyon sides would allow.

From the summit, he could see the sun setting in the west, but the valley was in deep shadow. Casey could see the white blur of his T-shirt. He took off one of his shoes and set its toe pointing toward the shirt. Of Mandy, there wasn't a sign.

*Well*, he thought. *I'll use the flashlight to get to the shirt and head straight down. Mandy'll be in a line from there. I hope.*

Rubbing his hand along his arms, Casey thought of the day he'd got the sunburn and wished he could feel even a little of that heat now.

Where was Dr. Norman? It had to be two hours since he'd dropped them off. Casey sat on one of the folding chairs and put up his feet on the other. He wished Mandy were sitting beside him. Not a sound. No voices. No birds. Nothing.

The sky at his back was darkening now, and the valley, black. Casey could see no sign of his white shirt.

Why, he wondered, hadn't he and Mandy been content to just sit and talk? Now he was sure to be in trouble again, like he had been last year when he'd gone out on his own to the Old Willson With Two L's Place and almost died. His dad would about give up on him after this, and the Normans would blame him for Mandy's setback. And he hadn't been any use spotting the crooks.

He remembered a saying of his grandmother's. "I feel like crawling into a hole and pulling the hole in after me." *That's exactly how I feel*, Casey thought.

A car's motor toiled in the distance. Casey sighed, brought his feet down from the second chair and stood up.

The light Dr. Norman had in the Jeep was powerful, but his cellphone wasn't working. He wasn't keen that Casey should go alone down into the valley, but he agreed to it when he realized Mandy couldn't answer his calls, and only Casey knew where she was. He gave Casey a big grey sweatshirt to put on and tucked a blanket under it to cover Mandy. Casey rolled back the sleeves, grateful for the warmth of the long shirt that went almost to his knees.

Casey put on the shoe he'd left pointing toward Mandy. He was on his way down as Dr. Norman, driving off to get help, turned his jeep and purred down the road from the summit roundabout. Quiet settled in again. Casey was grateful for the bright circle of light helping him see ahead.

*I should spot the T-shirt soon*, he thought as he eased carefully down the irregular slope. *Am I going too far to the right?* he wondered, for there wasn't any sign of his white shirt and the surface of the cliffs seemed different. It occurred to him that the way down had been much easier this time.

He swung the light around. To his surprise it showed something he recognized. "The cave," said Casey. "The darn tourist cave. I'm miles off course."

"Mandy! Mandy! Wake up and answer me, Mandy!" he shouted.

He knew there'd be no answer but he kept calling anyway. Casey sat down at the cave entrance and tried to remember how far the cave was from the route they'd taken down.

"Now," he said, "how would Dad handle the situation?" He knew perfectly well that his father wouldn't have got into this situation in the first place. Never mind that; how would he get out of it? "Think," he told himself.

"Well, point one: I am much too far to the right. Point two: The cave is roughly parallel to my T-shirt so I must edge to the left till I spot it. Point three: Get to the T-shirt and head down to Mandy."

Not that easy. Trying to move left on the level was much harder than going up or down, or being on the path to the cave. Every time he came to a fissure he had to work his way up to where it started and come down the other side. He was glad for the light, but holding it didn't make climbing any easier. He felt panic rise up.

"They'll be here soon with a stretcher and I won't be with Mandy."

Then, almost as if his dad were right beside him, Casey heard, "Steady on, son, you're doing fine." Swinging his light way to the left, Casey caught sight of a glimpse of white and side-stepped toward it. Mandy should be in line below the white shirt. She was.

With Dr. Norman's light fixed shining uphill, Casey took the blanket from under the grey sweatshirt and tucked it around the sleeping Mandy. A damp clay smell filled his nostrils and he pulled the sweatshirt close around him. He sat down beside Mandy and found her cold hands and rubbed them till they felt a little warmer. He shivered and looked up to summit of Horsethief Canyon.

"Thank goodness," he whispered.

Headlights ringed the summit edge and powerful lights moved down the cliffs. He could hear voices now, coming down toward him.

*They'll take care of Mandy. She'll be okay now. My part's over,* he thought. *All I have to do now is climb back up, get a ride to town, and get to bed so I can be up in time for work. It's sure not fun anymore; it's work!*

# CHAPTER THIRTEEN

For two weeks after their misadventure at Horsethief Canyon, Mandy had to stay close to home. For the most part Casey kept her company.

They talked about everything those long summer evenings.

"How're you getting along with that Trevor guy?" Mandy wondered.

"We just ignore each other most of the time, but the other day when I went to buy that new book on Chinese dinosaurs I've been telling you about, we actually had a conversation. He is totally into palaeontology." Casey thought for a minute and then said, "He's not so bad."

They didn't speak for a while as they sat watching the evening light fade and the faint stars began to show.

Then Mandy asked, "You got a girlfriend?"

"Well," Casey hesitated and then said, "I really like Marcia Finegood, but we're just good friends, like you and I are, and anyway, she's hooked up with Terry Bracco now." He didn't say anything for a while. Then, "There is a girl I really like an awful lot — Mary Kelly. She's the daughter of my parents' best friends, Maureen and Mike. We used to vacation with them every summer at their big lakeside cabin in southern B.C. She and I grew up together in a way, and we're always on the same wavelength. I was hoping to see her this year as well, but with all the construction at home and me being down here and Maureen and Mike taking a cruise, it looks like it's not going to happen. But you never know, it just might."

Casey turned to Mandy, "I sure won't miss Mary's brother, Jason. Mary and I can't stand him since he turned eighteen — like, I mean, he is a real jerk — but I will miss Mary. We text message a lot, so we know what's going on in each other's lives, but it would be so great if we could spend some quality time together. Like I say, there's just a hair of a chance we could go out there for a couple of days.

"But, enough about me. How about you, Mandy? Got someone special?"

Casey saw Mandy blink a couple of times, but it was ages till she said, "There used to be — a terrific guy named Sam — but since we moved down here, I've heard from him only twice, and my Edmonton friends tell me he's going steady with Lacy Lord."

"Lacy Lord! I can't believe it," Casey shook his head. "I know her; blonde, and …?"

"Well-endowed," Mandy smiled.

"Yeah, very well-endowed. Great swimmer too, of course, but not everyone's fave as I recall."

"Anyway, since Sam, nary a one. Except you, of course, but as we agree, we're connected by friendship, not romance."

Mandy yawned. "Time to call it a night, Casey. See you tomorrow."

Casey rode his bike to work every morning, carefully locking it to the rack in front of the museum, and he'd taken a few rides around town on his own. But it wasn't as much fun as when Mandy was riding alongside. They played a lot of video games, listened to a lot of music, watched a lot of movies, and played chess. Casey's grandmother had taught him well, and Mandy knew the rudiments.

An unexpected visit from Casey's favourite brother, Hank, and his current girlfriend, Sarah, made the kind of break Casey needed — it was perfect.

Casey realized he hadn't told them about buying the mountain bike. *I mean,* he thought, *it's my money.* But he knew how his dad loved to be consulted about things, and he wished he'd asked his advice or at least told him. He needn't have worried. The chief superintendent, who loved every wheeled vehicle ever built, approved of Casey's purchase. He thought the bike was wonderful. So wonderful, in fact, he asked if he could try it out. He was so tall his knees came way high as he pedalled, but he checked out all the gears and came back full of praise for Casey's choice.

There were other good parts to the visit, too, like the evening meals and get-togethers at the Normans'. Both sets of parents got along very well.

But as Casey'd expected, his dad was pretty upset at what had happened to Mandy in the canyon, and was waiting for Casey at the museum door the last afternoon of their stay to walk back to the Normans' with him.

"Honest, Dad, going to Horsethief Canyon was Mandy's idea." He stopped walking, scuffed his right shoe, and looked up at his dad. "I admit that heading for the other side of the canyon was mine; but Mandy wanted to go — she really did."

"Mandy's older and should have been more sensible," said Chief Superintendent Templeton, "and it certainly isn't your fault that she fell, but you've got to learn not to take unnecessary risks when it's someone else's well-being that's at stake."

"I'll try," Casey said, hoping that was the end of the lecture. It wasn't. His father started talking again.

"I have to say that you really used your head in Mandy's rescue; Bill Norman is most impressed with that and, as I've told you before, with your detailing your encounter with the thieves."

*Hurray for Dr. Norman!* Casey shouted to himself.

"And," Casey said out loud, "we're not doing anything the least bit strenuous now."

"Good," said his dad. "Now let's get back for supper."

Everyone had a great time at supper that night and the food was terrific. Mandy, of course, had to have liquids only because of her recuperating throat. During dessert, Casey's mother turned to him, "Terry and Kevin say 'Hi,' and Mike said to remind you about the contest. What contest?"

Casey grinned, "Oh, I'll tell you about it sometime."

But then and there he realized he'd not been doing any real exercises — just walking and biking, and certainly not any arm-strengthening ones. *Better get back to it,* he thought. *It'd be real embarrassing if Mike beat me.*

"And there's more news," Casey's mother continued. "The Ogilvies and the Maitlands are taking Bryan and Greta on a Baltic cruise next week."

"I'm so pleased for them," Casey said, straight faced. "Wish I could go along. *Not.*"

As he and Mandy were walking slowly up and down the Normans' street the day after his parents' visit, she said, "You seem kind of different when your dad's around, Casey. I wonder why."

Casey was quiet for a few steps, then said, "Well, when I was growing up I hardly saw Dad at all. He was always on some mission — first with an RCMP mission in Bosnia, to train Bosnian police, and then with the same sort of mission in Afghanistan. That's where he was pretty badly wounded and decided to leave the force. He'd been with it long enough to retire anyway." He thought for a minute and added, "We're getting to know each other better now. I guess you could say we're 'bonding.'"

# CHAPTER FOURTEEN

Casey was so bored with sitting for hours every day at the museum he could hardly wait to get out of there at night. He'd been keeping an eye on Trevor and caught him more than once looking over the artifacts on Casey's desk. Casey developed a placement system, so one day, when he came in and saw that things were not as they should be, he knew right away that a couple of bone fragments were missing.

What to do? Though they were from a selection he hadn't categorized yet, he knew how many had been on his desk, but not which ones weren't there now. Looking up, Casey spotted the camera above the museum entrance. He was sure its range reached as far as his desk. When he finished work, he'd ask security if he could have a look at its footage of the afternoon. He'd do it without implicating Trevor, just say he wanted to see how much the camera saw.

The day dragged on. He couldn't read, of course, because he had to work and watch the door. There hadn't been any visitors even remotely like the two he'd seen back in June. He was convinced the conspirators' plans had changed and they weren't coming back. Dr. Norman and the security staff thought so too, but asked Casey to stay till the middle of August, just in case.

Casey did get to see the surveillance camera video that evening. He'd made an appointment with the head of security, who worked out of the administration office, and was let into the building as it closed for the night. He took care not to be seen by Trevor, who was busy serving a customer who couldn't make up her mind. Pretending to be looking at the tape to see if the suspects were on it, Casey was actually hoping to get a look at Trevor taking stuff from his desk. At one point there was a "whooshy" moment on the tape as someone's arm whipped across the camera's range. It could have been Trevor's: it could have been anybody's.

*I'll have to catch him in the act,* Casey thought, deciding he'd better not accuse Trevor without proof.

The next day, Casey dabbed red marker on the back side of all the samples left on his desk. Then he set his plan into motion. The next time when he signalled for security to hold the crowd while he went to the washroom, he didn't. He stood flat against the bend of the corridor leading to the washrooms and waited.

He saw Trevor dash across from the Gift Shop and scoop up a handful of fragments from Casey's desk. Casey darted out and grabbed Trevor's wrist. Trevor tried to wrench his arm free but Casey held on firm.

"Drop them, Trevor," he whispered. "Drop them and bring back the others you've taken."

"Yeah," Trevor sneered. "Or what?"

"Or," Casey said, "you'll lose your job."

"Your word against mine, Casey," Trevor hissed, as he dropped the samples back on Casey's desk. "Like who's going to believe a know-it-all newcomer like you? I'll just say you took the stuff yourself."

"You want to take the chance?" Casey asked. "Just look at your palm."

Trevor stared down at his open palm. It was a mass of red marks. Casey picked up one of the pieces Trevor had dropped and showed Trevor the red marking on it.

"You swear you'll bring back the stuff you stole and I won't call security. Otherwise I will, right now."

Trevor was so furious he turned dark red. He was muttering to himself as he crossed to the Gift Shop and went in. Casey followed and saw Trevor take out a key from his pocket and unlock a side drawer of his desk. He reached in, gathered up a big handful of specimens, then walked over and dumped the pieces into Casey's open hands. One fell. Trevor gave it a little kick with the toe of his right shoe, and walked away.

# CHAPTER FIFTEEN

By the first week of August, Mandy was well enough to go for long walks after the museum closed. She and Casey covered every inch of Drumheller. Casey knew every dinosaur statue on every corner of the town. By the week before Casey was to leave, Mandy was well enough to bicycle again.

"Let's explore somewhere new," Casey suggested after work on his last Friday. The Tyrrell had closed early because there was to be a huge international reception that night. "We won't go up any hills or down any valleys or anything, just follow a couple of side roads — see where they go. I'm really sick of seeing the same streets over and over."

"Should be all right," Mandy agreed. "Some of the guys I've met at the swimming pool live just east of town; the land's pretty flat out that way. These guys bike in a lot so it can't be all that far. I'm pretty sure I know how to get to their area and I'd like to see them; find out what they did all summer."

"You lead the way," Casey said.

In twenty minutes they were out of town; in twenty more they were lost. They were on a gravel road now. Casey was glad for all the gears on his bike; it made biking on the rough surface so much easier.

"This road's tough going." Casey was realizing how hard Mandy was having to pedal. "What say we push our bikes for a while."

Mandy agreed and the two walked slowly down the road. The only sound was the crunch of the gravel.

"Look over there." Mandy pointed to a field where several horses stood. "They look like Icelandic horses. See their long manes and see how short and sturdy they are?"

"I've never even heard of Icelandic horses," Casey said. "I didn't even know they had horses in Iceland."

"They've had them there over a thousand years," Mandy told him. "The Vikings brought them over and the strain has been kept absolutely pure. Once a horse leaves Iceland, it's never let back in."

"How do you know all that?" Casey asked.

"Saw it on a horse documentary on TV."

"Well, I don't know much about horses." Casey nodded his head toward the opposite side of the road, "But that herd of cattle are Charolais; my uncle raises them up near Richford."

"Really?" Mandy said. "I didn't know what they were."

They walked on in silence, slowing to stare when a red-tailed hawk landed on a fence post.

"It's real nice out here, Mandy," Casey said, "but do you have any idea where we are?"

"Not really," Mandy said a little uncertainly. "That turn we took a while back — maybe we should have gone straight on instead."

"See the old gate past that clump of trees up ahead?" Casey asked. "If there's a house there, we can ask the people how to get back to town."

The gate was locked and the house at the end of the driveway looked deserted.

"So, let's head back," Casey suggested. "Once we get to a better road there's bound to be traffic, and we'll signal someone for info on how to get to town."

"Listen," Mandy held up her hand. "Can you hear a car?"

"Yeah," Casey said. "It's on this road and it's coming fast." They just had time to scramble into the ditch when a dirty beige four-door zoomed past. It hit a bump in the gravel, flew up a few feet, crashed down, and stopped. The passenger door opened and a tall woman stepped out. A tall woman shouting in a man's deep voice.

"You stupid idiot! I should have known better than to let you drive!"

Another woman got out of the driver's side and said, also in a man's voice, "Oh, quit griping. It's not our car and I had to find out if I could really drive with this here fancy new leg."

"I know it's not our car, but it IS my back you about broke," the passenger said.

"You didn't break nothing," the second woman said, and added, "God, my head is hot." He grabbed off a blonde wig and threw it in the car window before they both got in again and drove toward the gate. The car stopped and the passenger got out to unlock the gate. She'd discarded her wig as well.

"My gosh!" Casey whispered. "It's them. I saw that pair at the museum this afternoon and I didn't rumble them. We gotta get back in one big hurry. If they've already got the stuff, they'll be out of here, like fast."

They got on their bikes and pedalled away from the house.

Just before the junction of the narrow road leading to the locked gate and a secondary road, Casey asked, "Right or left?"

"Right for sure," Mandy said. "Then it'll be right again when we reach the highway and we'll be going west and back to town."

Casey turned at the sound of a motor.

"Looks like our two friends. Let's keep riding."

The car slowed and stopped a few metres ahead of them. The window was open and the driver said, "What're you two doing out here?" It was the voice of the former "passenger."

"Heading back to town," Mandy answered.

"That's a long ride," the speaker said as he got out of the car. Casey could see that the men had discarded their dresses and were in jeans and T-shirts.

"We'll take you. We can tie your bikes on the back of the car."

"No thanks." Casey shook his head. "We're out to get some exercise."

"Get in," said the man, opening the rear door.

"Like I said, no thanks," Casey said firmly.

"You don't hear so good," said the other man who was still in the car. "He said, 'Get in.'"

Mandy and Casey laid their bikes in the ditch and climbed reluctantly into the back seat.

Nobody said anything as the car drove off. At the first crossroads the car made a fast U-turn and sped back the way it had come.

"Hey!" Casey shouted. "We've got to get back to town!"

"You're not going back to town, you dirty little spies," said the driver. "We saw you coming out of the trees by our drive. Don't know what you're up to, but you saw too much."

"Yeah," the second man agreed. "You won't get hurt if you behave yourselves, but we can't have you blabbing about seeing us dressed as women."

"Our job will be done by tomorrow morning," said the driver, "then we'll be gone. Someone will likely find you one of these days. In the meantime," he turned the car sharply into the drive and through the open gate, "in the meantime, you'll be our 'guests.'" He cruised toward the low, weathered house.

"And don't try anything," the other man said. "You may have noticed we're bigger than you, and we really know how to hurt people."

He sat in the car as the driver opened the door, grabbed Mandy's arm, and pulled her out. Making a lunge for the open door, Casey felt a huge hand grab his shoulder and squeeze.

"Yeow!" Casey shouted.

"I said not to try anything."

The hand squeezed harder as the car door was slammed shut from the outside by the man holding Mandy. Casey heard a "click."

"The doors are locked now," said the man in the front seat.

A dozen questions flashed through Casey's mind.

*What's the first guy going to do to Mandy?*

*How are we going to warn Dr. Norman about tonight's break-in?*

*What are we going to have for supper?*

*Will we ever be found?*

*What is Dad going to say about me getting into trouble again?*

*Why aren't I being taken into the house with Mandy?*

The last question was answered first as the man who'd taken Mandy came out the front door and walked to the car. The man in the front seat clicked open the doors. Casey was grabbed roughly by the arm and dragged outside. He tried to pull away but the man's grip held firm.

"This way, kid," he said, hauling Casey, who was wriggling frantically to get free, toward a shed behind the house. The man opened the door and pushed Casey onto the floor and slammed the door with his foot.

"Pull out your shoelaces and hand them up." Casey did as he was told. "Now lie down on your stomach and put your hands behind your back."

The floor was covered with dirty straw. It smelled musty and Casey sneezed twice. He felt a shoelace cut into his wrists. The other one was whipped around his ankles and pulled tight. With his head flat on the floor, all Casey could see of the man was his black shoes.

"You may think," the man said, knotting the shoelaces, "there's no lock on this door, but just to save you the trouble of trying to get out, I'll tell you there's a couple of brackets out there for a two-by-four I'm putting across the door. So you're in here till you're found, and that ain't gonna be soon."

The door slammed shut again and Casey heard a thump as the two-by-four dropped into the brackets. Sitting up wasn't easy; Casey had to roll over onto his back, tuck his ankles under his body, and force himself up.

Light poured through cracks in the wall of the long, narrow, windowless room. At the far end of the room was a manger; on the walls hung assorted pieces of tack.

Casey pulled at the shoelace but it only cut deeper and deeper into his wrists.

*I gotta analyze this,* he thought.

*Point 1. I have to free up my wrists first.*

*Point 2. I have to undo the lace on my ankles.*

*Point 3. I have to put the laces back in my shoes.*

*Point 4. I have to get out of here.*

*Point 5. I have to …*

He stopped as he heard the sound of a car backing up.

*Point 5. I have to get Mandy free.*

*Point 6. We've got to let Dr. Norman know that tonight is the night for the break-in. That we're okay and he shouldn't be distracted looking for Mandy and me.*

Casey knew he had to find something to cut the lace. He made himself focus on each piece of tack, on every inch of the wall. There was nothing with a serrated edge or a sharp one.

Finding he could stand if he kept his knees bent, he hopped to the manger and, backing up to it, put his tied hands over the rim and felt among the dried-up straw and oats. Nothing. As he dragged his wrists back, the shoelace caught on the rough edge of the manger.

"Worth a try," he said, rubbing the lace back and forth. He couldn't see if it was fraying, but he figured it might if he kept at it and pulled his wrists apart at the same time. At first, as the wood scraped the skin from his wrists, he felt like screaming at the pain.

"Something's giving," he said to himself. "I don't feel the wood anymore." He rubbed the lace furiously back and forth. His hands flew part. He rubbed his wrists, then bent to free his ankles. Blood from his wrists ran down his hands and onto the lace, making the knots slippery and hard to undo.

"At last," he said, turning to pick up the pieces of the other shoelace. He tied the frayed ends back together and put the laces in his shoes.

"Okay, Point 4. Get out of here."

Taking in every part of the cobwebby walls, Casey walked slowly around the room, concentrating on the side with the door. He stopped and stared. Level with his chest he saw the point of a nail. Three inches below was the point of another nail. Five feet along and parallel with the first two nails were the points of two more nails.

"They've got to be the nails holding up the brackets for the two-by-four. Okay. Now how can I pound them out?"

He took off his high-top sneakers and banged on one of the nail points. It went right into the rubber and left his shoe hanging on the wall. He looked around. An old bridle hung by a buckle. Part way down the bridle was a tarnished circle the size of a large coin. Casey gave it a pull, but it was riveted on. He pulled the bridle free and took it over to where his shoe was hanging. Holding the bridle with the metal disc over the top nail point, Casey hit it with his shoe. He looked. Light shone through the nail hole. Another wallop with his shoe on the metal over the lower nail point and he heard one end of the two-by-four crash to the ground. He pushed at the door, but it wouldn't open. He used the same technique on the other two nails and heard the two-by-four fall to the ground.

Casey opened the door and rushed for the house.

Inside there wasn't a sound or a sign of Mandy.

"Mandy!" he shouted running from room to room. No answer. "Mandy?" Casey stopped and listened. Still no sound. "My God," he said, "What if they've kidnapped her?"

Casey began opening doors. "Mandy," he yelled as he found the basement stairs behind the first door. "You down there?" He almost slid down the steps to a cellar, completely empty except for a large furnace.

"She can't be in there; door's too small."

A door from the kitchen opened to a pantry, empty except for a half case of red wine on a waist-high freezer. The wine was so heavy Casey almost dropped the box as he set it on the floor. Fearing what he might find in the freezer, Casey hesitated, then pulled up the lid. In the freezer were a few frozen dinners.

Outside the bathroom, another door opened to a large linen closet, its shelves stacked with bed linen and towels. On the floor, a heap of soiled clothes moved as Casey was about to shut the door. Casey tore at the heap.

"Oh, Mandy."

Bound and gagged, Mandy was struggling to get free. The cord around her wrists was so tight her hands were almost marble white.

Casey took out the gag.

"My gosh, Mandy, those guys are monsters."

"It was awful under there," said Mandy, her voice hoarse. "I couldn't get free, and I thought no one would ever come for me." This was a scared side of Mandy Casey hadn't seen before. Casey quickly undid the cords that tied her wrists and ankles and rubbed the deep pressure marks.

"Where did they put you?" Mandy asked Casey. Her voice had a real rasp to it.

*I pray this won't be another setback for Mandy,* thought Casey.

"In a horse barn out at the back," Casey told her. "Tell you all about it later. We have to find a phone."

"I heard them talking on one," said Mandy, as they went from room to room.

"Must have been a cell," said Casey, "there's no phone here."

"We have to find a way to tell Dad," said Mandy. "Wonder how near the next farm is?"

"We sure didn't see another house along this road," said Casey. "Let's go past the gate, and back to the road where our bikes are. I don't think you're up to riding back to town, but we have to alert the museum somehow." *All that boring effort sitting watching people come into the museum,* he was thinking, *all for nothing.*

They'd barely reached the gate when, from far to the north, they heard a droning and saw a small plane low above the horizon.

"I'll bet that's the crop duster," said Casey, pulling Mandy back toward the house. "It usually makes several passes. Get three sheets." In the pantry, Casey pulled out four wine bottles; Mandy followed him out to the road with a load of sheets.

"We'll make an S.O.S.," yelled Casey, grabbing a sheet from Mandy.

In minutes, they'd spread the three sheets side-by-side along the road, weighing down the corners with field stones. Casey cracked off the top of two wine bottles with a rock and handed one to Mandy.

"Print a huge 'S' on that end sheet; I'll do this one." Together they poured an "O" in wine on the middle sheet and waved frantically as the slow plane flew over them and went on.

"He didn't see it," said Casey.

"Guess not." Mandy looked totally discouraged. Then she yelled, "Hey, wait! He's turning around!"

# CHAPTER SIXTEEN

"Move, Mandy!" shouted Casey. "He's landing right on the road."

The small biplane came barrelling toward them and stopped in a huge cloud of dust about ten metres away. At first, they couldn't even see the plane through the cloud of dust it kicked up, but as the engine slowed to a halt they saw ahead of them a shiny yellow, single-engine biplane. Its shape looked old-fashioned but the plane itself looked new. Casey had seen pictures of a similar plane in his father's photo album of his early days as a young Mountie up north.

By the time Casey and Mandy reached the plane, the pilot, wearing a beat-up leather jacket, had climbed down and was pulling off an ancient leather helmet and old-fashioned flying goggles. Hacking and wheezing from the dust, he began fanning his face with a brilliant white scarf. Casey couldn't decide which was older, the man or the plane.

"He can't be for real," Mandy said under her breath, "but I'm sure glad he's here, ghost or not."

"Times like this," the man said, his cough turning to a laugh that seemed to let the sun shine through the dusty air, "I could almost be persuaded to get me one of them glass bubble things for over the cockpit." The laugh stopped as quickly as it had started and the pilot stood in front of Casey and Mandy, hands on his hips and a stern look on his face.

"You two had better have a good reason for that S.O.S.," he said. "That's a sacred sign, to be used only in real emergencies. They call me Mad Dog, and I don't take kindly to being made a fool of."

"We're Mandy and Casey," said Casey, "and we have a very good reason for signalling you. We desperately need your help, Mad Dog," Casey went on. "Here's why." He gave Mad Dog a point-by-point summary of what had gone on and what was about to happen.

"I've lived a long time, done some far-fetched things, and heard a lot of wild stories," Mad Dog said, shaking his head, "but what you've told me is one of the wildest tales I've ever heard."

"But it's true, Mad Dog, honestly," Casey said earnestly. "Every word of it is true, and we need your cellphone to call the museum."

"Don't have one," Mad Dog told him, "but this is your lucky day." He climbed up and reached in the plane for his radio.

"I'll get hold of the local RCMP and tell them what's going down," he said. "If I know that Mountie crew, they'll be on the situation in minutes." He pressed a button and tried the mic. Nothing. He pressed it again and tried the mic. Nothing.

"Gol'darn thing!" He threw the radio back in the plane. "Looks like your luck has started waning. I've been meaning to get that blasted thing fixed."

"What'll we do now?" asked Mandy.

Casey turned to the pilot. "Can you take us back to Drumheller?"

Mad Dog thought for a minute, his eyes fixed on a point somewhere in space.

"I have enough gas," he said, "but I don't have enough space. Not for both of you. You can see this Jackaroo's now a two-seater, with that tank sitting where two other seats used to be."

"You go, Casey," Mandy said. "You know better what the men look like and you'll be more use. I feel rotten. I'll stay here. There's a bed in the house I can lie down on. I'll rest till I'm rescued."

"At least you'll be more comfortable than you were in Horsethief Canyon," Casey said.

"Right," Mandy agreed.

"Listen," Mad Dog said, "if that car left a half hour ago, they'll get to the museum before we can, what with my having to land at my strip way out of town."

"Couldn't you track down their car before they get to town?" Casey asked. "I'm pretty sure I could spot it."

"Now, that's an idea." A big smile lit Mad Dog's grizzled face. "If there's one thing I'm good at, it's finding something and buzzing it. We'll find them, then we'll figure out what to do about it."

"I'll hoist you up to the right-hand seat, Casey. Good-bye Mandy."

Mandy walked as far as she could from the road as Mad Dog gunned the engine. Clouds of dust billowed up. By the time the dust cleared, the plane was well on its way. Mandy waved. The end of a white scarf flowing out of the cockpit waved back.

# CHAPTER SEVENTEEN

"So, your name's Casey." Mad Dog pointed for Casey to put on a pair of earphones and a microphone and adjusted his own set. "Casey what?"

"Templeton," Casey said.

"Again?" asked Mad Dog.

"Templeton," Casey spelled it out. "T-E-M-P-L-E-T-O-N."

"Thought that's what you said." Casey felt Mad Dog staring at him and looked over into his eyes.

"Any chance you're related to Constable Colin Templeton, RCMP?" asked Mad Dog. The engine sound was just a dull roar.

"My dad's Chief Superintendent Colin Templeton, RCMP, retired," Casey answered.

"He ever serve up north?" Mad Dog asked.

"Yeah," Casey said, "when he was first in the force he was stationed at Fort Smith and Fort Resolution."

"Well, I'll be darned." Mad Dog was smiling. "Gotta be the same guy."

They were flying quite high and Mad Dog said, "Casey, I'm going to try something with the radio, you take the controls."

"Me?" said Casey. "I don't know anything about flying."

"Just grab the controls and keep her steady," said Mad Dog. "I'll take over if anything goes wrong."

Casey couldn't believe it. He was actually flying a plane. The wind pulled hard at his hair and the sun almost blinded him, but here he was, actually flying a plane. It was so easy.

"Tilt her a little to the left," Mad Dog called out. "Not so much! *Not so much!*" Mad Dog grabbed the controls; as he did, the radio crashed to the floor. "Okay, Casey, take her again."

*I never want to land,* Casey was thinking. *This is so great.*

"Well" — Mad Dog sounded frustrated — "the stupid radio's shot for sure. I'll take over now. Our only hope is to get a bead on that car."

He swooped down and was flying so low Casey was sure he was going to hit telephone lines.

"You know, you look like old Colin," said Mad Dog, "and that report you made to me in point form? Exactly like how he made reports."

Mad Dog was silent for a while then continued, "You say he's retired now? Don't see how he could ever retire. He was such an eager beaver. What's he do? Play golf and sit around watching TV?"

"No," said Casey. They were above a secondary road now; the only car on it was a shiny green RV. "Dad's mayor of Richford and he's on a federal commission dealing with hate problems. He doesn't have time for just sitting, let alone golf — says it takes too long."

"You ever hear him talk about me?" Mad Dog asked Casey.

"Not by the name Mad Dog," said Casey.

"How about Harry Thirst?" asked Mad Dog.

"I've heard that name, and I've seen a picture of Dad and someone that might be you in front of an old plane."

"I know that picture." Mad Dog was smiling. "That was my 'Kaydet' — that's what they used to call the Boeing-Stearman PT 17s. Had her converted to a crop-duster a long time ago. Flew that Kaydet 'til I bought this one a couple of years ago — only Tiger Moth Jackaroo in Canada, all the rest are in South America and Australia. It's multipurpose, this here Jackaroo — got a crop-dusting tank up front and these two seats so I can give flying lessons and take people up for rides."

He grinned. "I used to get in your dad's hair with that old Kaydet. But there was one day he and I brought medicine to a dying Dene. Just like Wop May and Vic Horner had done about fifty years before. We were friends that day."

"So that *is* you in the picture with him?" Casey asked.

"Yeah. Like I said, we were good friends that day."

They flew in silence for a while. Casey could see the juncture of the secondary road and the highway. On the highway, Casey spotted what he was sure was the car.

"Mad Dog," he shouted. "That beige job just ahead. I think that's it."

"We've gotta be perfectly sure," Mad Dog shouted. "I'll go right down beside it and you take a look in the window."

Casey couldn't believe a plane could get that low; he could see tiny cracks in the concrete.

"It's them! It's them!" he shouted. An arm with a gun at the end of it came out the car window and fired: twice. One bullet tore into the top right wing of the plane, just missing Casey. Mad Dog pulled up the nose of the plane and made a slow circle above the car. He passed the radio up to Casey.

"Casey," he shouted. "I'm going down again, right over the car. When I don't see any other cars on the road, I'll pass over the car real low to shake up the driver, and when I shout, you drop the radio on the road in the path of the car. They're bound to swerve and maybe even leave the road. Don't drop it till I shout. When I say 'Now!' let 'er rip."

The car under them was swinging from side to side on the four-lane stretch of highway; Mad Dog was following a little behind. Casey could see another car, a van, approaching the thieves' car from the opposite direction. Mad Dog'd have to wait till it passed. He chose his moment, lifted the left wing so Casey would have a clear view, swooped over the car, and shouted "NOW!"

Already leaning out, Casey dropped the radio in front of the car. The radio smashed into a million pieces and the car just rolled over it.

"Oops!" Mad Dog shouted as he upped the nose of the plane and let the car get ahead again.

"Got anything else I can try?" Casey shouted.

"Grab that flare down there," Mad Dog pointed behind his seat. "I'm not sure what'll happen if it's dropped, but if it goes off, it'll sure distract them."

When Mad Dog signalled, Casey dropped the flare. It didn't go off; it didn't break up; it just rolled harmlessly to the side of the road. Mad Dog tilted the plane up again.

"Are we out of options?" Casey looked over at Mad Dog and was surprised to see him smiling.

"Not quite," he said, reaching for a metal cylinder, "this here's a fire extinguisher. Unscrew the cap and when I fly low over the car again, spray it on the windshield."

Casey readied himself, and when Mad Dog was in position pressed the spray nozzle. Thick white foam flew back all over him, missing his face by a hair.

"Aim lower," Mad Dog shouted, getting into position again.

This time, Casey, with Mad Dog flying sidewise, and just over the car, leaned as far down as he could, and pressed the button again. The thick white foam covered the windshield, and the car swerved into the ditch. Casey looked back. The car was nosed into a large wooden sign.

"All right!" Mad Dog yelled gleefully as he turned the plane south, gunned the motor, and headed toward Drumheller. "That'll put 'em out of action for now."

Casey could feel the plane picking up speed.

"I'll be at my airstrip in a few minutes," Mad Dog said. "My van's at the end of the runway and we'll be back at Mountie headquarters in about ten minutes."

"Awesome," muttered Casey as they streaked toward Drumheller. "Awesome."

# CHAPTER EIGHTEEN

Of all the people Casey didn't expect to see as he and Mad Dog rushed into Drumheller RCMP headquarters, his father topped the list. But there he was with Dr. Norman and a group of officers.

"Where's Mandy?" said Dr. Norman as Casey walked in, "and where have the two of you been?"

"Mandy's okay, Dr. Norman. I …" Casey began.

"Casey," his dad interrupted. "What are you doing with that man?"

"Hold everything," said Mad Dog with an authority Casey wouldn't have expected, "until you hear what Casey has to say. He has major news and he's just been through a very traumatic experience."

"Okay, Casey," said Dr. Norman.

*This is a real test,* thought Casey. *Where'll I start?*

"Okay. Point One. Like I said, Dr. Norman, Mandy is okay, but her throat hurts again. She's resting in a house east of town; I can take you there later." *I hope I can take you there later,* he thought.

"Later? Why not right now?"

"Point Two," said Casey. "By absolute chance, Mandy and I came upon the two I've been watching for — the ones I heard talking about robbing the Tyrrell. They were dressed as women, and I'd actually seen them earlier in the day. We heard them saying that tonight is the night for the robbery."

"As you all know, tonight's the Tyrrell's big Donors' Reception," interrupted Dr. Norman. "Honoured guests from all over Canada and the U.S. — the whole world — are invited. It's a black-tie affair, by invitation only, and the invitations will be checked against a list. Can't see how anybody could crash it, but steps have to be taken in case. Every Tyrrell security guard will be on duty; we've even hired a few extras."

"Point Three," Casey continued.

"Never mind the darn points," said his father, "get on with it!"

Casey looked at this dad in surprise and plunged in.

"We started back to find a phone when the two men who'd gone into the house came after us and forced us to leave our bikes and get in their car. They said we were spying on them and that they couldn't take a chance letting us go because we'd seen them dressed as women, and we might have heard what they'd been saying. Which, of course, we had. Anyway, like I said, they forced us into their car, a beige four-door, and took us back to their place.

They locked Mandy in the house and me to a horse shed at the back."

"Take a breath, Casey," said Dr. Norman. "I have to call Mandy's mother; she's frantic with worry."

"Here, Casey." Casey drained the glass of water his dad handed him and, as soon as Dr. Norman was back, he went on. "There was no phone at the place. Mandy and I started out to get our bikes and ride to find a phone when we heard an airplane motor. I figured it was a crop-duster, and Mandy and I printed a big S.O.S. on three sheets with red wine. Mad Dog landed on the road, and when he heard what was up, he tried to radio you folks here; but his radio wasn't working, so he and I flew up to try to spot the car before it got into town. Mandy went to lie down at the bad guys' hangout."

"And?" three voices spoke as one.

"And when we found what I thought was the car, Mad Dog flew down so I could check through the window...."

"Through the car window?" Staff Sergeant Striker asked in amazement.

"Well, yes." Casey sounded as if it were the most natural thing in the world.

"I'm not surprised," his father said, shaking his head.

"Well," Casey went on, "the driver fired some shots at us so Mad Dog tilted up the plane's nose, circled, came in low, and gave me the radio to drop in front of their car."

"I watched; there were no other cars near," Mad Dog said defensively.

"I'll bet you did," muttered Chief Superintendent Templeton.

"The radio smashed to pieces, a flare I dropped rolled away, but the fire extinguisher foam I sprayed on the windshield caught the driver off guard and he swerved into the ditch." Casey beamed with pride. "He crashed right into a billboard. Once we were sure they weren't going anywhere, we flew to Mad Dog's airstrip and came directly here."

"How about the men?" Casey's father asked. "Were either of them hurt?"

"Well, we couldn't stop to see, of course," Casey said. "But you'd better have an ambulance go out with you, just in case."

He turned to Mad Dog. "How far out of town are they?"

"Well, they were already on the four-lane, and that begins about ten kilometres from the city limits," Mad Dog said.

There was silence for a minute as the group absorbed what they'd heard. Then Staff Sergeant Striker said, "Burnster and Harley, over to the Tyrrell. Opel, call up an ambulance and alert the hospital. Jackson, two cars outside, now. Slater and Jeffries, head out east with Jackson. Chief Superintendent, will you come out in my car with Casey and … Mad Dog?"

To Casey's relief, his father said, "No thanks. I'll go with Dr. Norman. You'll be taking your own car, Bill?"

"Yes," Dr. Norman said. "We'll follow the others out."

In the back seat of Striker's police car Mad Dog said, "Your father wasn't exactly happy to see me, Casey, was he?"

"Well, no," Casey agreed, "but he didn't come in this car to protect me from you or anything like that."

No," Mad Dog considered. "No, he didn't, did he?" After a couple of minutes, he said, "We should be there, Striker."

"Yep," said the staff sergeant, "I see the other police car and the ambulance. Thank heavens we'll have daylight for long enough to assess the situation." He made a U-turn and pulled up behind the ambulance.

"Are the men badly hurt?" Casey asked Constable Jackson, who was standing by the overturned beige car.

"Who knows," Jackson replied. "There's nobody in the car or anywhere around here."

"They must have been okay enough to get out and hitch a ride," said Striker, picking up his telephone. "Harley? The two men have abandoned their car. Could be on their way in to the Tyrrell. Jackson, Slater, and Jeffries are on their way there."

Dr. Norman had pulled up across the highway and he and Casey's father were walking toward the wreck.

"They've gone, Chief Superintendent," the staff sergeant said. "Jackson, Slater, and Jeffries are heading back to the Tyrrell in case the perps got a ride and are going to follow through on their plan. If they did get picked up, they'll likely have stolen the car by now. We'll be on the lookout for the driver. Could be they've stashed him somewhere."

"Casey, were they dressed like women when you last saw them?" his father asked.

"No, Dad," Casey said. "They'd changed into men's clothes. But I didn't see any of the women's clothes they'd been wearing when I was looking for Mandy, or the wigs, so they could have taken them in the car."

The staff sergeant was on the phone again. "They could be dressed as women, Harley."

"If they put on those ladies' things, you'll have trouble spotting them," Casey said, leaning into the window of the staff sergeant's car. "Unless they talk, you'd swear they're women."

Into the phone, the staff sergeant said, "We'll be bringing along an eyewitness to the Tyrrell, but we have to go back to headquarters first." Putting his cellphone in his pocket, he asked, "Will you and Casey come back to headquarters with me, Chief Superintendent? I'd like your input on how we can best use Casey."

"Of course." Casey's father got into the front seat as Casey got into the back.

"Mad Dog," the staff sergeant said, "can you find the house where Mandy Norman is?"

"Sure," said Mad Dog. "It's right beside Grindley's field where I was dusting."

"Okay, you take Dr. Norman there, and the ambulance will follow in case Mandy needs to be taken to the hospital. All right, Dr. Norman?"

But Dr. Norman was already crossing the highway.

# CHAPTER NINETEEN

Back in Mountie headquarters, Striker and Casey's father were deep in conversation. Casey sat in an armchair in a corner, his arms dangling, his head thrown back against the cushioned chair top.

What a day! Images of the whirlwind hours passed before his closed eyes. Terrible moments like when he thought he couldn't escape; chilling moments like when he thought Mandy had been kidnapped; numbing moments like when he heard shots and saw bullet holes in the airplane's wing.

*Mandy!* he thought, hoping she was all right. *That dirty gag couldn't have been good for her throat, and the way they tied the cords round her wrists? If I hadn't got to her when I did, the circulation would have been totally cut off. What a miserable pair of crooks!*

"Casey, wake up! Casey!"

Casey opened his eyes. Striker was standing over him, his father a few feet away.

"How's Mandy?" Casey asked.

"Really pretty well, considering," said his dad. "The ambulance did take her to the hospital, but the doctors there released her after they'd examined her throat."

Casey sighed with relief, sat up, and stretched. "Gosh, I'm glad about that," he said.

"Duty calls now, Casey," said his father.

"What the heck is that, Dad?" asked Casey, looking at a black garment his father was holding up. A black, woman's garment. "You're kidding," he said. "I have to wear that?"

"You do," said his dad. "Those two men know you, Casey. One tied you up. They'll spot you in a minute."

"The company catering the party at the Tyrrell loaned us the smallest waitress's uniform they had. Try it on."

Casey pulled the uniform over his T-shirt and pants.

"Fits not too bad," the staff sergeant said. "Now try these." He handed Casey a pair of low-heeled black flats.

Casey untied his sneakers and pulled them off. He tried forcing his heavy tube socks into the shoes.

"They'll fit if you wear these." Striker handed Casey a square plastic package.

"Tights?" said Casey. "I have to wear girls' tights?"

"I'll show you where you can shower and change," the staff sergeant said.

The shower felt good. Trying to get the slippery black nylon uniform over his partly dried body didn't. It kept sticking to the damp parts. Casey put on his shorts, tore open the package of tights and held them up.

"How the heck?" he said out loud.

He tried putting the tights on standing up.

"It can't be done," he said. "How do girls ever do it? I swear it can't be done."

Casey spread his damp towel on the floor of the shower room and lay down on it. He got the left leg on okay. When he'd got the right leg pulled on, he found he twisted the tights somehow and he couldn't stand up. He took the right leg off, twisted it around, pulled it over his foot, and up his leg.

"All right," he said. Standing up, he found he had about eight inches of extra tights at the top to deal with. He folded the elastic over and down. His feet slid easily into the shoes. He gathered up his T-shirt, pants, and socks and went back to the staff room.

"You look fine." Casey's dad was trying not to laugh. "You'll look even better with this."

He centred a blonde wig on Casey's head.

"And you'll look even better with these." The staff sergeant fixed a white cap on Casey's wig and tied a tailored white apron around his waist.

"He still looks too much like Casey," said the chief superintendent.

"How about I wear a pair of glasses?" Casey suggested. He was getting into the situation, realizing how heavy his responsibility was going to be.

"Wait a sec." The staff sergeant walked over to a tall filing cabinet and opened the bottom drawer. "Lost and Found," he said, taking out three pair of glasses and handing a gold-rimmed pair to Casey.

"Way too much distortion," said Casey, "I can hardly

see anything."

"Try these," Striker said. Casey took a pair of rimless glasses from him.

"Yikes. These are worse."

Casey put on the last pair: big ones with blue plastic rims and little rhinestone butterflies at the top corners.

"They're okay," he said. "What do you think?"

His father and the staff sergeant both nodded.

"Go take a look at yourself," said his dad.

In the shower-room mirror, Casey was surprised to see a shortish, blonde, very nice-looking waitress with fancy blue-rimmed glasses.

"I need lipstick," he said, coming back into the staff room.

"Right." Striker crossed again to the lost and found drawer. He and Casey's dad opened half a dozen lipstick tubes.

"Blondes like you should wear pink," said his dad.

"Yes, they should," Striker agreed. "Come here. I'll put it on for you."

"Now you're really ready." His father nodded, satisfied. "Go take a quick look."

"Now I'm really ready," Casey agreed, smiling into the mirror.

·

# CHAPTER TWENTY

"The plan's this, Casey," said Striker. "We three will go in a back entry to the Tyrrell. By the time we get there, all the guests will have arrived and had their invitations checked against the master list. Your job will be to pass among the guests with a plate of food or a tray of drinks; someone will be ready to hand you a full plate when yours gets low so you won't have to go back to the kitchen."

"If you see anyone suspicious," Casey's father took up the instructions, "report it to the nearest museum guard or to a Mountie. If only one man is spotted, he will be kept under close surveillance until the other one is found."

*It's a good party,* thought Casey as he wove through the crowd with his tray of hot hors d'oeuvres. As the champagne flowed, the decibels rose; the guests were enjoying themselves.

*Who wouldn't be happy with all this food!* Casey had never seen such a buffet spread. He didn't know every dish, but with his mother being such a fabulous cook, he recognized a lot of them. "Hope there's some left for me when this business is over," he muttered to himself.

"Here, take these around, now." Someone took Casey's plate and handed him a round tray of full champagne glasses. He thought he'd have trouble balancing it but found he needn't have worried; in one minute flat, all the full glasses were gone and the tray held only empty ones.

Someone took his tray of empties and gave him another full one. Casey walked among the guests, looking intently into their faces and smiling as he passed them a new glass or took their empty one. People smiled back at him and one man pinched his bum as he passed.

*I can't believe that happened,* he thought, and stopped smiling.

Casey looked at his watch. Two hours? He'd been walking round for two hours. "I'm tired and my feet hurt," he said to himself. "I've just got to take off these shoes for a few minutes. Putting his tray of empties on the floor away from the crowd, Casey caught a glimpse of himself in a glass display case. His wig was crooked, his lipstick smeared, and his tights bunched around his ankles. He slipped out of his shoes, grabbed the seat of his tights and pulled hard. Too hard. He felt something give and looked down. "Oh no!" he said right out loud. Instead of wrinkles, he saw one of the legs of his tights separated completely from the top.

Casey rolled down the tights and pulled them off by the toes. He scrunched them into a stringy black mess and pushed it down the front of his uniform. He looked at his reflection.

"Looks like I've got a tumour." He pushed the stockings first to one side and then to the other. "Won't do," he said looking around.

*Tyrannosaurus rex* towered majestically above, his gigantic feet among stones. "Stones," said Casey, as he rolled up tights and tried to tuck them under some stones. The stones were cemented down. He looked toward the lobby and saw Trevor crossing from the Gift Shop.

"Trevor, come here," he hissed, beckoning him over. Trevor stared at Casey, not recognizing him at first. Then the light came on as he walked over.

"What's going down, Casey?"

Casey handed Trevor the bunched up tights. "Something big," Casey said. "Stash these and I'll tell you all about it later."

Trevor looked down at the black tights now in his hands.

"Better be one good story." he said as he walked back to the Gift Shop, stuffed the tights behind some cartons, and walked back to the lobby.

Casey forced his swollen feet back into the black flats and picked up his tray of empties. He found a spot where he could watch the assembled guests, now listening attentively to speeches of welcome and thanks. He studied each face. In the back row he saw a man, a man in a tuxedo as were all the other men, who looked somewhat like the one-legged crook. But this man was so much stouter. Casey looked along the rest of the back row. When he looked back to check the stout man once more, there was no sign of him — but there was a museum guard at the very back of the area.

*I'll tell him,* thought Casey as someone took the tray of empties and handed him a tray of after-dinner chocolates shaped like different dinosaurs. Casey made his way along the wall to the back of the crowd. He got there just as the speeches ended. Several people turned to see what he was carrying. As one of them reached for a chocolate, he pushed Casey's elbow and fifty small chocolate dinosaurs scattered on the floor.

Casey could feel the guard watching him as he picked up the candy. *He could give me a hand,* Casey thought. One dinosaur was right at the guard's feet. Casey reached for it and froze. Then, picking up the last dinosaur, he put it on the tray with the others and threaded his way to the kitchen.

"Where's my dad and the staff sergeant?" Casey asked Constable Jackson.

"In the chef's office back there, Dr. Norman's with them." He pointed to a closed door halfway down the kitchen. Casey ran to the door and flung it open.

"One of them is the guard standing at the back of the crowd."

"Show us," said the staff sergeant, as he and Casey's father hurried to open the kitchen door a crack.

"The one with the moustache," said Casey.

"See him, Jackson?" said Striker. "You and Jeffries go round to the front door. Keep out of sight, but keep him in your sight. Harley, you watch him from here."

"How about the other man, Casey? Any sign of him?" asked his father.

"I saw someone I thought might be him," said Casey, "but he looked too fat to be the one-legged guy. When I looked back to check, he was gone."

"Dr. Norman," said Striker, "can you take us to where your most valuable portable artifacts are without going through the crowd out there?"

"Just follow me."

Dr. Norman led the way through a maze of corridors. Casey had a hard time keeping up to the three long-legged men. Dr. Norman pointed to a door.

Sergeant Striker stopped in front of the door and said, "If our man is in there, will you" — he nodded to Casey's father — "give us a hand apprehending him?"

"Sure," Casey heard his father reply. Somehow, Casey figured, this was not an unfamiliar situation for his father.

Dr. Norman beckoned Casey to look as he silently opened the door to a long, narrow, shadow-filled room and walked up to a slim man who was holding a glass-cutter above a display case, a long black bag hung in front of him suspended from a cord around his neck. A museum guard was on the floor, a hypodermic needle sticking right through his uniform into his arm.

Dr. Norman closed the door again, opened his cell-phone, pressed a number, and said, "Paramedics by the internal route to Display Room Number Four and an ambulance to the back entrance ASAP."

He opened the door again and walked up to the thief. "Good evening. Is there something we can help you with?"

"It's him," Casey whispered, and Staff Sergeant Striker and Chief Superintendent Templeton walked up to the man, each taking one arm.

"Dr. Norman," said the staff sergeant, "would you be nice enough to tell the officers watching the 'guard' in the foyer to take him into custody?"

"With the greatest of pleasure," said Dr. Norman. "Come, Casey, you deserve to be in on the final chapter."

Casey made a quick detour to the Gift Shop to get Trevor. *After all,* he was thinking, *Trevor's been in on the "watch" since it was first set up.*

They circled the attentive crowd, getting to Dr. Norman's office just as the guard Casey had identified from the back of the lobby was brought in in handcuffs. The thief with the glass-cutter was already there, also in handcuffs. His jaw dropped as Casey came in.

"Why, you little creep!" he shouted. "Somebody's going to get you for this."

"I think not," Sergeant Striker said.

# CHAPTER TWENTY-ONE

Mandy was sunning on a chaise; Casey was swinging in a hammock. They were in the Templetons' big back yard, admiring the handsome addition his parents had added to their house while Casey was away.

"Your bedroom's the one with the walk-out deck?" asked Mandy, looking upward.

"It is *so* great," Casey smiled. "I can sleep out there any time I like."

"And you say the whole single-storey addition is your grandmother's suite?"

"Yeah," Casey said. "You know, she's coming to stay with us for good now. Before it was decided she couldn't live on her own anymore, Dad built a terrific place for her there," he pointed to a row of tall windows on ground level. "Grandma didn't like it much, so now I get it; and they have the upper storey with a balcony."

"What about Hank and your other brothers?" Mandy wanted to know. "They still come home sometimes, don't they?"

"Once in a while, but, really, they're hardly ever here," Casey told her. "So Dad got smart and turned the front part of the upstairs into three little rooms, one for each of them; works out fine."

"You ever hear any more about Mad Dog?" Mandy asked. "Dad tells me the museum bought him a very fancy radio. And, by the way, did you know it was Mad Dog who found our bikes and helped Dad tie them on our car while I was riding away in the ambulance?"

"Yeah, I heard," Casey said. "I really like the old guy, and I know my dad does too, deep down. Dad told me the whole story of what happened between the two of them. You know my dad served up in the Northwest Territories about thirty years ago, when he was first in the Mounties?"

Mandy nodded. "I heard it mentioned."

"Well, my dad's job was law and order, and Mad Dog, who flew all over the North, wasn't a fan of either. He drove my father absolutely nuts with his escapades and his capers and his wild flying stunts. Dad admits Mad Dog was the best of the latter-day bush pilots. He says Mad Dog was skillful and he was fearless; he also says that he was reckless. He'd do anything. And once, when they needed someone to fly medicine to a really remote place in terrible weather, Mad Dog and my dad did the mission together. They got to be friends."

"I'll bet Mad Dog buzzing that car with you in his plane put a lot of pressure on that friendship," laughed Mandy.

"It did," Casey said. "But you know, my dad's been down to see old Mad Dog a couple of times since then, and Mad Dog took him for a long ride right over Calgary. Mad Dog's a pretty lonely guy since his wife died and there aren't many around the area who have any idea what his background is."

"Glad to hear it's working out between them," Mandy said. "Think I'll tell my dad to drop in on him sometimes."

She yawned. Casey yawned back. Silence filled their space.

Casey was thinking back on the summer — the good and the not-so-good parts. It was good the bad guys got caught and that he'd justified all the money the Tyrrell had paid him; good that the museum had asked him to come next summer as a digs helper; good that he and Trevor had got to know each other.

*I'm sure glad Trevor'll be going to the University of Calgary to study palaeontology*, Casey thought. *I might like to do just that in a couple of years*.

It was also good that Hank and Sarah were still an "item," and that Hank was doing so well in computer sciences; good that he and his dad were getting along — were friends now, Casey figured; good he and Mandy had really got to know each other; good that he had a great big new room.

And the bad? Bad that he'd done some dumb things and would have to pay for them with lots of hard work this fall; bad how the "contest" with Mike had gone — not well, he had to admit. They'd set up a two-out-of-three arm wrestling contest at the Snick Snack café. All the kids were there. Casey won the first round: Mike the second. It was all very exciting until Mike, in a swift, powerful move, pinned Casey's arm to the table.

*He won "hands down,"* Casey thought, *"arms down" anyway. Oh well.*

Bad he'd missed the mid-August barbecue. Everyone said it was wonderful. Next year, he hoped.

A call from his mother broke Casey's meditations.

"Will you give me a hand with these trays please, Casey?"

He rolled off the hammock and took a tray of cookies from his mother, who put another tray, with a big pitcher of iced tea and three glasses, on a table beside Mandy.

"Looks great, Mrs. T.," said Mandy. You shouldn't have gone to the trouble."

"Nonsense, Mandy," Mrs. Templeton replied. "After the hospitality your folks showed Casey and showed us, it's the very least I can do."

As they drank their iced tea, Casey's mother asked, "So, Mandy, what are the doctors saying about your throat? Will you be able to start swimming again soon?"

"Soonish," Mandy told her. "I'll work out a little in the local pool first. The doctors think I'll be able to get back on St. Hilda's swim team around Christmas, and early in the new year start to swim with Swim Calgary."

"Terrific," said Casey's mother. "Now, I've got to get back to work — getting everything ready for Mother is a daunting task." Her cellphone rang.

"This'll likely be Mother."

Mrs. Templeton flipped open her cell.

"Hello." With a nod at Casey, she mouthed, "Your father." She listened for a while, then said, "Oh really. Are you sure?" Another pause, "He's right here, I'll ask him.... Casey, Dad wants to know if you'd like to go to the Kellys' cottage for Labour Day weekend? He has to stay in Ottawa so it'd be just you and me?"

"I'd love to go," Casey beamed. *What a way to end the summer*, he thought.

"Yes, Colin," his mother was saying, "Casey and I will fly down to Penticton and drive south to the Kellys' from there. We'll miss you. No, Mom's not coming until the eighteenth, and, yes, Hank will be here till then. Bye for now."

"Didn't think that'd happen," Casey said.

"Nor did I," his mother replied, "but I have to tell you I'm going to welcome a nice peaceful break from all the goings-on around here."

She leaned over to pick up the trays.

"I'll bring them in later, Mom," Casey said

"Okay," his mom said. "See you, Mandy."

"See you, Mrs. Templeton," Mandy said.

They were quiet till Mandy said, "So, you'll have that visit with Mary you were hoping for."

"Yeah," said Casey, "that is so cool. What about you, Mandy?" he asked. "You ever hear from that Sam guy?"

"Yeah, I heard from him," Mandy's voice took on a firm tone. "Apparently Lacy Lord dumped him for a swimming instructor; so he came crawling back to me. Correction. He tried to come crawling back to me. I just hung up on him."

They were quiet again until Mandy said, "Amazing how that whole business at the Tyrrell worked out, isn't it, Casey?"

"It really is." Casey pulled a canvas captain's chair nearer to Mandy. "No wonder that famous collector who put the plan into operation is so rich — he is one smart guy. To give his invitation to one of his men so the guy could get into the party and take the stuff he and his partner had already cased."

"They know who the collector is," Mandy told Casey. "My father says all the invitations were gone over and the one the thief used was identified. Word is going out to the palaeontological circles here and in the States to steer clear of him."

"It's no wonder that one-legged guy looked so stout." Casey stood up and shoved a pillow under his T-shirt. "With a glass cutter and a suction cup to pull out, and all the other tools he had — and that huge padded bag for the cut glass and all the stuff he planned to steal. They figure he'd have left the tools, just like artifact poachers do once they get what they want; that way he could take as much as possible in his 'stomach.'"

"And that other guy, the guard?" asked Mandy. "How did that work again?"

"Well," said Casey, "the first time I heard the two men talking in the Hoodoo, the lame one was telling the other how he'd got to know several of the museum guards. I gather he got to know one of them, a guy who lived alone, pretty well; knew where he lived and everything. On the morning of the robbery, they parked near his house, called him over as he left for work saying they'd give him a ride. Instead, they knocked him out, drove to the back of his house, used his key to get in, locked the guy in the basement, and took one of his fresh uniforms."

"They were busy boys that day," Mandy said, moving her chaise out of the sun.

"You know it!" said Casey. "They used the guard's house as a base that whole day. Got dressed in their women's wear and came to the Tyrrell from there to double-check what they wanted to steal."

Casey shook his head. "I still can't believe I totally missed them."

"Then," said Mandy, "they went to the country where we were to clear out their rented house."

"And put us out of action," Casey added.

"I hear they stole a kid's car after you and Mad Dog sprayed their windshield."

"Right," Casey said. "The kid stopped to pick them up. They overpowered him and drove him to the guard's house."

"Where," Mandy and Casey said together, "they locked him in the basement with the guard."

"That's where they got ready for the party," Casey said. "Talk about masters of makeup. The guy who played the guard? He plucked his bushy eyebrows to be the woman and added a moustache to be the guard. With the guard's hat on, I didn't recognize him at all, and the other guards must have thought he was one of the extra guards hired for the night."

"But you knew his shoes, I hear," said Mandy.

"I knew his shoes," said Casey. "I really knew his shoes. I'd had time to examine them when he was tying me up on the floor of the horse shed. They had a different sort of stitching around the sole."

"Did you ever hear what they used to knock out that guard?" Mandy asked.

"Dad told me it was a very powerful solution of sleeping medication. He didn't wake up until the next morning."

They lay there in companionable silence. Casey was so happy Mandy had come for a day's visit. Before Casey had come home, he and Mandy had planned to spend time together when they could. No romance here, they agreed, but very good friends who'd shared a summer neither would forget. So many exciting happenings.

*For me*, Casey was thinking, *the very best thing is the museum giving me lifetime ownership of the tooth Mike and I found. It will still be in the museum collection, of course, but it will have my name on the card beside it. To think, our two pieces are the whole tooth after all — except for a tiny bit they say we'd never have found anyway.*

Casey looked up to the bright blue sky through the green leaves of the giant elm tree. High among the branches, the leaves of one small branch were bright yellow. Fascinated, he watched as one golden leaf detached itself and floated down in easy circles. It landed on his chest. Casey looked at it. He picked it up. He looked back up at all the other leaves on all the other trees.

*They too will all become golden*, he thought. *They too will all flutter down and land on something. They too will all have to be picked up. By me.* He shook his head and looked up again at the blue and the green, and the gold. *Might as well enjoy the view till then.*

# ABOUT THE AUTHOR

Poet, painter, and writer of children's fiction, Gwen Molnar is the author of three poetry collections for children, *I Said to Sam*, *Animal Rap and Far Out Fables*, and *Just Because, A Collection of Light Verse and Nonsense*, as well as three Sebastian first chapter books, an early chapter book, *No Presents Please*, the first Casey Templeton Mystery, *Hate Cell*, and *Hazel's Rainbow Ride*, with Barbara Hartman as illustrator. She lives in Edmonton, Alberta.

# FROM THE SAME SERIES

**Hate Cell**
*A Casey Templeton Mystery*
Gwen Molnar

Casey Templeton has recently moved with his family to the southeastern Alberta town of Richford. While out one night, he makes a frightening discovery — a sophisticated office filled with computers, a printer, and racist posters and flyers! Richford is harbouring a cell of vicious white racists who are targeting everyone they deem "alien." Casey leads an investigation into a warped world where hate is marketed on the Internet and innocent people are preyed on by bigots and bullies blinkered by their own prejudices.

Available at your favourite bookseller

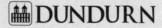 DUNDURN

Visit us at
Dundurn.com | @dundurnpress
Facebook.com/dundurnpress | Pinterest.com/dundurnpress